The Conspiracy

Even the book morphs!
Flip the pages
and check it out!

Look for other **ANIMORPHS**®
titles by K.A. Applegate:

The Conspiracy

K.A. Applegate

AN
APPLE
PAPERBACK

SCHOLASTIC INC.
New York Toronto London Auckland Sydney
Mexico City New Delhi Hong Kong

Cover illustration by David B. Mattingly

ISBN 0-439-07031-7

12 11 10 9 8 7 6 5 4 3 2 1   9/9 0 1 2 3 4/0

Printed in the U.S.A.
First Scholastic printing, July 1999

The author wishes to thank
Laura Battyanyi-Wiess
for her help in preparing this manuscript.

For Bill Battyanyi

And for Michael and Jake

The Conspiracy

CHAPTER 1

My name is Jake.

Just Jake.

My last name doesn't matter.

Where I live and go to school don't matter, either.

What matters is that we're in a war, fighting for the survival of the human race.

You're thinking *Yeah, right.* That's okay. I know — I probably would have said the same thing once.

No way. Not a chance. If it's true, then where are the troops storming the beaches? Where are the bombs? Where's the battlefield? The RPVs and cruise missiles?

Well, it's not that kind of a war.

The battlefield is wherever we are, we being my friends and I. We are animal-morphers, given the ability to absorb DNA by touch and then morph into that animal. It's an incredible weapon, the kind that both dreams and nightmares are made of.

Ask Tobias, who stayed in his red-tailed hawk morph longer than the two-hour limit and now spends his days catching and eating small mammals.

Or check in with any one of us in the small hours between night and morning, when the nightmares come, the nightmares of twisting bodies and mutating minds.

Like I said, this is not your standard-type war.

We're the whole army, the six of us. We get some help from the Chee, but they are incapable of violence, so when it comes to the down and dirty, we're it. Us, alone, against an alien empire that has already terrorized the galaxy.

Yeah, I know. Nice odds.

Most of us learned to fight the hard way in a deadly, on-the-job-training-type deal.

But some of us had a head start, like my cousin Rachel, who loves it all. And Ax, whose full name is Aximili-Esgarrouth-Isthill, warrior-cadet and younger brother to Elfangor, the Andalite who gave us the power to morph before he was murdered by Visser Three.

I know, sounds like bull, right? Sounds like maybe I need to spend some time in a rubber room.

But it's true. Every now and then the crazy becomes real.

And this is not a clean war, if there is such a thing. I mean a war like World War II, where thousands saw the wrongs being committed and stood up to correct them. Where you attacked an enemy you could see, an enemy who wore a uniform and came right back at you, guns blazing.

This isn't that kind of war at all.

The Yeerks are more subtle than that. They aren't predators, they're parasites. They don't want to destroy humanity, they don't want to make big piles of bodies, they need our bodies in one piece to continue their invasion.

See, they're basically slugs. Parasites. No arms, no legs, no face. Blind.

That's why they need host bodies.

They slither into your ear, seep into the crevices of your brain, open your memories.

And you're still inside yourself while it's happening, trapped, helpless, begging for the nightmare to end.

Only it's real. And it doesn't end.

You want to warn people and you can't make the words come out. But the Yeerk in your head can hear them. It can hear your pitiful cries, your impotent threats. It can hear you beg, *Please, please leave me, please get out of my head, please*. . . . And it can feel you slowly surrendering even the pretense of resistance.

The Yeerks are everywhere, using their involuntary human hosts to move freely, to recruit new members into their cover organization called The Sharing with promises of good, clean, wholesome family fun.

They're the ultimate enemy.

We've identified a few of them, though.

Our assistant principal, Mr. Chapman.

My best friend Marco's mother.

My big brother, Tom.

I know how the guys fighting in the Civil War felt, North against South, brother against brother.

Living with the dark, ugly fact that if you met your brother on the battlefield, he would kill you.

Unless you killed him first.

I know the real Tom is still inside himself somewhere, raging against the Yeerk holding him hostage, begging for someone to save him.

I know because I was infested once by the same Yeerk who'd first infested Tom before his body had been turned over to a new Yeerk. I had access to its memories, so I saw how Tom had been dragged, screaming, fighting, and finally pleading to the Yeerk pool to receive his slug.

I was saved. Tom was not.

But it stays with me, that memory. It always will.

So will the battles. Win, lose, or draw, they're chaotic clashes full of pain and rage. And when the fighting's over and the adrenaline drains away, you're left exhausted and sick, with way too many memories.

My grandpa G — "G" for great-grandpa — told me something once, way before I ever could have understood what he'd meant.

My family had driven eight hours to visit him in his cabin in the woods. He and I were sitting on the dock at the lake, watching the fish snatch mosquitoes off the water's glassy, mirrored surface.

And it was so quiet.

Quiet enough to make me wish I was home with the TV blasting and my dog Homer gnawing on a rawhide chew.

I was about to leave when Grandpa G said, "You know, I see myself in you, Jake. You've got an old soul."

An old soul? Was that supposed to be good or bad?

He never said. Just gave me a small, kind of sad smile, and looked back out over the lake.

I hadn't known what he'd meant then, or why he'd said it. I don't know, maybe he saw my future, somehow. Because now I was old. You see too much pain and destruction, you get old inside. It's one of the by-products of war.

I'm the unofficial leader of the Animorphs. I send us into battle. When things go wrong, when we get hurt or have to run for our lives, that's on me, too.

I'm not complaining. Has to be done. You know? Someone has to make the calls. A good leader has to make tough, informed decisions. Recognize his soldiers' special strengths and use them accordingly. Fight to win with the knowledge that he may die trying.

But most important, a leader won't ask anyone to do anything he wouldn't do himself.

That one came home to haunt me.

Because in three days, my brother Tom was either going to kill or be killed.

And it was up to me to decide.

CHAPTER 2

I came around the corner after school and saw a taxi parked out in front of my house.

My mother shot across the porch, suitcase banging against her knees, and hurried down the sidewalk to the cab.

What the . . . ?

My mom didn't take cabs. Nobody around here did.

Everybody had cars.

"Mom!" I yelled, jogging over. "What happened?"

Because something had definitely happened.

I mean, I've seen my mom sniffle at Save the Children infomercials and Hallmark cards, but I can't remember the last time I ever saw her really cry.

But she was crying now.

Something must have happened to Tom.

Or to my dad.

My knees went weak and wobbly.

Funny, how even when your whole life has shifted into a daily *Twilight Zone* episode, there are still some things that can make you panic.

"I left you a note on the fridge, Jake," she said, hefting her suitcase into the trunk and slamming it shut. "My flight leaves in an hour and the traffic —"

"Mom, *what happened*?" I blurted.

My voice was high and shrill, not exactly the voice of a fearless leader, as Marco would have pointed out, had he been there.

"Oh." She blinked away fresh tears. "Grandpa G died. His housekeeper, Mrs. Molloy, found him this morning. I'm meeting your grandparents and we're driving out to Grandpa G's cabin to make the funeral arrangements."

"Grandpa G's dead?" I echoed, trying to wade through the emotions whirling around in my head.

Grandpa G. Not Tom. Not my father.

"Yes. His poor heart just gave out," she said.

"You're going to the cabin?" I said. "What about us?"

"You'll be coming out as soon as your father

clears his work schedule," she said, touching my shoulder, forcing a brief smile, and sliding into the backseat. "He'll tell you about it. Everything will be fine. Make sure your suit is clean. I'll call when I get to Grandma's. I gotta go, honey."

She slammed the door and waved.

I watched as the cab disappeared around the corner.

Now what?

I headed into the house. Checked the scrawled note stuck under an apple magnet on the fridge.

Yeah. Grandpa G was dead.

According to Mrs. Molloy, who'd talked to the doctor, his heart had stopped while he was putting jelly on a slice of toast. He'd never even gotten a chance to eat it.

I shivered.

I'd cared about Grandpa G and now he was gone, and my family was smaller.

I didn't like that.

The kitchen door burst open. Tom stormed into the room.

"And I'm telling you, Dad, I can't go!" he snapped, tossing his books onto the table and scowling at me. "What're you looking at?"

"You're home early," I said, surprised.

My father plodded in, weary, harassed, and closed the door behind him.

"So are you," I said, glancing from him to Tom. "Did Mom tell you guys about Grandpa G?"

"Yes," my father said. "I was hoping to get here in time to take her to the airport but the traffic was terrible. I saw Tom walking home and picked him up."

"Did you know we're supposed to go out to the cabin?" Tom demanded, glaring at me like it was somehow my fault.

"Uh, yeah," I said cautiously, trying to figure out what his problem was. "So?"

"So, Tom's already informed me that he doesn't want to leave his friends to attend his great-grandfather's funeral," my father said, looking at Tom, not me. "However, he doesn't have a choice. We're going. All of us."

"When?" I said, feeling like I was missing something important. It was there but I just couldn't grab it.

"We're driving up Saturday morning," my father said.

"Dad, I can't," Tom insisted. "The Sharing's expecting me to help out this weekend. I gave them my word!"

"Well, you'll just have to explain that something more important came up," my father said. "I thought The Sharing was about promoting family values, right? Well, we're going to pay our respects to Grandpa G as a family."

10

"Dad, you don't understand!" Tom argued desperately.

Why was Tom so dead set against going out to the lake?

Okay, so it was boring. Grandpa G's cabin was the only house on the lake. His closest neighbor had been Mrs. Molloy and she lived seven miles away, halfway to town.

The only other house around was an old, abandoned hunting lodge across the lake.

No cable. No Taco Bell. No streetlights or crowds.

No movies. No malls. . . .

No Sharing. No Yeerks. . . .

"Uh, Dad?" I said. "How long are we staying?"

"It depends on the funeral. I'll write notes so you'll be excused from school through Tuesday of next week —"

"What?" Tom's eyes bulged in shock. "Tuesday? Dad, no way! Four days? I can't stay away for four days!"

"You can and you will," my father said, losing his patience. "We're going as a family and that's final."

Tom's throat worked. His hands clenched into fists.

And for one brief second I had the crazy thought that he was going to attack my father.

11

And oh, man, even though I couldn't morph in front of them, I could feel the surge of adrenaline that comes right before a fight.

Three, maybe four days. The maximum time a Yeerk can last without a trip to a Yeerk pool is three days. Four days without Kandrona rays and the Yeerk in Tom's head would starve.

Starve, Yeerk. Starve!

"It won't be that bad, Tom," I heard myself pipe up. "The lake's nice, remember?"

It broke the stalemate.

Tom looked at me. "You're an idiot, you know that?"

He was playing his role as condescending big brother. I was playing my role, too.

Starve, Yeerk. Die in agony, die screaming, Yeerk!

"Shut up," I said. "I'm not the one who's being a big baby about leaving."

I said it to annoy him and to bring us back to the rhythm we knew, the kind of normal sniping I could handle.

Because the hatred in Tom's eyes when he'd looked at my father had scared me.

And the hatred that had flared up in me, the hatred of the Yeerk, the sick thrill of anticipating its pain, had scared me, too.

"That's because you have no life," Tom sneered.

"Oh, right, and you do?" I shot back.

"More than you'll ever know," he said darkly, distracted now.

"Enough," my father said. "I'm going to change. When I get back we'll order pizza. How does that sound?"

"I'm not hungry," Tom muttered, staring at the floor.

I wasn't either but my father was looking at me expectantly, so I said, "Pizza. I'm there."

My father nodded, satisfied, and left.

I gave my brother a look of sympathy, making peace. "Maybe you can get out of it, some way."

I had to fight to keep the sneer off my face. *Or maybe, Yeerk, your cover is falling apart, maybe you'll have to choose between keeping Tom and keeping your filthy life.*

"Shut up," Tom said absentmindedly. The Yeerk had no use for me, no interest in me. I was dismissed. Irrelevant.

I turned and blasted out into the backyard, my mind already buzzing with the possibilities.

Tom's Yeerk was trapped. Under pressure. Squeezed. It wasn't ready for this turn of events. Didn't know how to play it out. Didn't know what to do.

An opportunity? Maybe. Yeah, maybe.

Die, Yeerk!

13

CHAPTER 3

Supper was awful.

Tom tried everything to get out of going.

He begged. Pleaded. Complained. Sulked.

He even tried reasoning.

My father didn't budge.

I finished supper and bolted. I needed to think about what was gonna happen and I couldn't do it with Tom around.

I hit the sidewalk, automatically heading for Marco's, but I really didn't know where I was going.

I wanted to talk to Cassie, but she and her parents, both vets, were at some animal rescue seminar until later.

Too bad, too, because she was the one I really wanted to talk to.

Out of all of us, Cassie's the one who really understands the more complicated things: motives, emotions, right and wrong.

Marco's my best friend, and if I wanted to talk about what works, about how to get from point A to point B and forget the consequences, I'd talk to Marco.

But Cassie sees beneath the surface. I'm no genius, but I knew I was too close to this to see clearly.

"Yo, Jake man! I was just on my way over to your house." Marco. Jogging toward me. "I need your English notes."

I looked up, startled. "Oh. Uh, hi."

"What'd I do, wake you up?" he said, body-checking me.

I shoved him back. "Since when did you start saying 'Yo'?"

"I was going to yell 'Hey, handsome,' but I thought you might prefer 'Yo.'"

"Uh-huh."

"So, yo-yo, what's up?"

"I was just thinking about something," I said, shrugging. Then I decided what the heck. Marco's been my friend since we were in the sandbox. Plus, he'd lost his mom — complicated

15

story — so I figured he'd know how I felt. "My Grandpa G died today."

"Man. Too bad," he said, falling in beside me as we headed back to my house. "He was old, though, right? I mean he was in World War III."

"World War II, Marco. Two."

"No, duh," he said. "We spent a really unpleasant afternoon in the middle of World War II, you may recall. Or at least some time-distorted version of World War II."

Long story there, too.

"Yeah, he was in the war. The real war," I said as we rounded the corner to my house. "My mother flew out to help with the funeral arrangements. We're supposed to —"

My father's car wasn't in the driveway.

Odd.

"When's the funeral?" Marco said.

"I'm not sure. Probably Monday," I said, walking a little faster. The deep, dark part of my brain, the part that sensed danger, was already dumping adrenaline into my blood.

Something wasn't right.

"What?" Marco asked, instantly catching my mood.

"Don't know. A feeling."

A feeling like there was something important I'd forgotten. And because I had forgotten it . . .

I tried to shake it off. I walked faster. "I'll be

out of school Monday. Maybe Tuesday," I said absently, crossing the front lawn. "Me, my dad, and Tom are driving out on Saturday morning."

"That's what, four days?" Marco said, then grabbed my arm. "Four days without Kandrona rays?" he said in a low, tense voice. "Does Tom know how long you're gonna be gone?"

"Yeah, he and my dad had a big fight about it," I said, tugging free. "My dad said he had to go."

And then Tom had looked at my father with black hatred.

No, not Tom. The Yeerk inside of him.

Controlling him.

Tom's hands, doubled into fists.

Poised to leap at my father.

"You left them alone," Marco said. Not an accusation. No blame. Just fact.

Like I said, Marco sees the line that goes from A to B. He'd already seen Tom's dilemma. And he'd seen Tom's ruthless solution.

I followed Marco's narrowed gaze.

My house was still.

Too still.

I bolted, stumbled up the steps, and threw the door open with a slam that echoed down the street.

CHAPTER 4

Silence.

The empty kind, when you know nobody's there but you.

"Dad?" I yelled anyway, running into the hallway. "Dad? Tom?"

No answer.

Heart pounding, I took the stairs two at a time.

"Dad?"

Looked in my parents' bedroom. In Tom's. In mine.

Neat — except for my room. Empty.

Which made me feel a little better, but not much.

"Jake," Marco said from right behind me.

18

"Yaaahh!" I yelped, going airborne.

"Sorry."

"Don't do that!" I said harshly, pushing past him and heading back down the stairs to the kitchen.

I swung around, searching the kitchen for something, anything that would tell me where they'd gone.

Cabinets. Sink. Glass jars full of cookies and pasta and coffee, lined up on the counter. Coffee machine. Refrigerator. Toaster.

Orderly. Nothing out of place.

I exploded.

Slammed against the side of the refrigerator. BAM!

One of the magnets fell off. The apple, which had been holding my mother's note about Grandpa G.

Only the second note, the one that had been tacked beneath it, was gone. Had someone taken it? Why, when it had the flight number and details about what to bring when we drove out?

The garbage.

Frantically, I grabbed the plastic can and flipped open the lid. Knelt and peered inside.

Lying crumpled atop the banana skins and the coffee grounds and the empty yogurt container was a wad of pink paper. Crumpled. I rose and smoothed it out on the counter.

19

The top of the note was the one from my mother with the flight information. At the bottom of that note was my father's handwriting.

Jake: Went to a Sharing meeting with Tom to explain why he can't help them out this weekend. Be back soon.
Love, Dad.

"Oh, God," I whispered.

My father hadn't thrown away the note. Tom had. He'd been covering his tracks.

Tom was taking my father to The Sharing.

But not so he could be excused from his obligations.

He was going to make our father a Controller. He would watch as they forced him to his knees and pushed his head down into the thick, sludgy Yeerk pool. He would listen to his pleas. Listen to his cries. His screams of horror and disbelief and panic. Listen and laugh.

No.

I started to shake.

I should have known. Should have seen it sooner. Marco had seen it, why hadn't I?

"We have to find them," I said, searching my mind frantically for a way to do it.

"How?" Marco said. "We don't even know where they are."

20

"Marco, this is *my father*!" I shouted, losing it. "I'm not letting them take him."

"Even if we find him, you may not have anything to say about it," he said quietly. "It might already be too late."

No, it couldn't be too late. Couldn't . . .

No. They wouldn't have my father. I was going to stop them. Even if it meant stopping my brother.

Any way I had to.

Marco re-crumpled the note and put it back in the trash.

Placed the apple magnet back on the fridge.

I stood there, frantic, vibrating with impatience, wanting to go, go, GO somewhere, anywhere, just *get going* and find my father.

"We have to cover our tracks, Jake," he explained. "We can't let Tom know that we know."

"Right, whatever," I said, hurrying toward the door.

I didn't tell Marco, but at that moment I just didn't care about keeping our secrets. I didn't care about saving the world. I was saving one man. The rest of the world could take care of itself.

There were some losses I wasn't willing to take, no matter what. I'd lost my brother. That was it. I wasn't losing anyone else.

"The Chee," I said suddenly.

I reached for the phone. Marco pushed the receiver back down. "Not from the house, man. Look. Jake. Jake, listen to me."

"What? WHAT?"

"You're the boss, Jake. You're the fearless leader. But not right now, okay? You're too messed up over this. Let me call the plays."

I knew he was right. I said nothing. I hated Marco right then. Hated him because he wouldn't have made the mistake I'd made. He would have seen . . .

Hated him because he'd already lost his mother and he knew what the inside of my head was like, because he knew I was scared and just wanted to cry.

"Come on, man," Marco said.

We went down the block to a pay phone to call Erek King. He's a Chee.

The Chee are a race of androids. Pacifist by design. But definitely anti-Yeerk. The ultimate spies. Our friends. At least as much as a nearly eternal machine can ever be a friend to a weak, short-lived human.

The Chee would know of any Sharing meetings scheduled.

"There's nothing scheduled," the human-sounding voice said.

"But there has to be," I said desperately, pacing the length of the stupidly short phone cord.

"Tom's taking my father to it! C'mon, Erek, please!"

"Jake, you know I would tell you if I knew," Erek said with calm regret. "Perhaps Tom asked for an emergency meeting to deal with this problem."

"Then how are we ever gonna find out where they are?" I said, glancing at Marco to see if he had any suggestions.

He shrugged, looking miserable.

I turned away, wanting to cry.

Fighting to get hold of myself.

Think, Jake.

If the Chee didn't know where the Yeerks were gathering, how were we supposed to know?

"Wait," I blurted. "Stupid! I don't have to find the Yeerks to find my father. All I have to do is find my father and we'll find the meeting. Should have thought of it."

"All right," Erek said cautiously.

"No, it's easy. He always carries a cell phone. I'll just call and ask him —"

"You can't," Marco and Erek both said at the same time.

"Why not?" I said.

"Jake, if you call and ask your dad where he is, and then the meeting gets broken up by us, don't you think the Yeerks'll put two and two together?"

23

"I don't care," I said, before I could stop myself.

The sympathy on Marco's face evaporated. "You're not getting me killed to save your father!" he snapped.

"There may be another way," Erek said, interrupting. "Give me the cell phone number. You hang up, dial the cell phone, and I'll tap into the frequency. You call but don't speak. If your father picks up, I'll analyze the auditory data and we may be able to determine his location."

I didn't look at Marco. Couldn't. "Good. Great." I gave Erek the number, hung up, and dialed my father's cell phone number.

It rang once.

Twice.

My hands were shaking.

Marco was staring at me, eyes narrowed. His body was tense, ready to snatch the receiver if I as much as opened my mouth.

I closed my eyes, willing my father to answer. Praying it wasn't too late.

CHAPTER 5

"Hello?"

Tom.

Tom had answered my father's cell phone.

My mouth opened automatically to respond.

Marco lunged, twisting the phone out of my hand.

Put it to his ear.

Watched me with dark, unreadable eyes.

I didn't move. I couldn't.

Because I couldn't believe what I had almost done.

If I'd said one word, just one, then I'd either have condemned my father to the Yeerk pool or I would have condemned my friends to death.

I couldn't stop shaking.

Couldn't get control.

Marco listened, then hung up the receiver.

"You'd better call Erek back," he said coolly, stepping away from the phone.

I nodded, too embarrassed to even look at him, too worried about my father to say something that would close the distance between us.

"I've analyzed the incoming data from the call and have narrowed it down to four possible locations," Erek said when I called.

"Four!" I blurted. We didn't have time to search four different places! "Where are they?"

"Well, factoring in the frequency strength, the cell phone towers that were activated, and background noise such as the sound of jet engines overhead, car engines moving slowly, human footsteps, and various other sounds, our analysis suggests they're in the northern section of town, roughly between the eight thousand and the fourteen thousand blocks north-south, and the six hundred and twelve hundred block east-west. An area six blocks by six blocks."

"What's in that area that could hold a meeting, even a small one?" I was grateful. I was also impatient. Frantic.

"Senior Citizen Center, a small strip mall with four stores, a small hardware store, and an auto-body shop. Plus, about seventy-five private homes."

26

I let out a curse. "Homes! We can't search seventy-five homes! Erek, I need more."

"There was a snatch of conversation. Just two words."

"What words?"

"'Normal hours.'"

"What?"

"'Normal hours.' Like the last two words of a sentence. Blah, blah, blah, 'normal hours,'" Erek said.

I had a sudden flash of him on the other end of the line. Would he be in his true android form, or wreathed in the perfect hologram that let him pass as a normal human kid?

"Eliminate the auto-body shop," Marco said. "That'd be noisy. Real noisy. If they're open, that is. Same with the hardware. Nails dropping, paint cans being shaken . . . It's the old folks' home or the mini-mall."

"Or one of seventy-five private homes," I said. "Erek? We need your best guess."

"I don't have —"

"Take a shot!" I yelled.

"The mini-mall. Four stores. Play the odds," Erek said.

"Get hold of Rachel. Get her and the others up there to the other locations."

I slammed down the phone. No time for thank-yous. There'd be thank-yous if we won this race.

"Mini-mall," I told Marco.

"What about the old folks? They'd have a main room. Stores wouldn't."

"'Normal hours.' Sounds like a store."

"Unless it's about mealtime, or visiting time at the old folks' home," Marco said.

"Let's go," I said.

We jogged back to my house. It was the closest, safest place with no one home.

I stripped off my outer clothing — getting down to bike shorts and a T-shirt. The kind of tight, minimal clothing we can morph in.

I focused my mind on one of the double-helix strands of DNA that swim in my blood.

When I opened my eyes, I was falling. Shrinking. And no matter how many times it had happened before, it still made my stomach lurch.

Smaller and smaller, with the floor racing up to slap me, falling like I'd jumped off a skyscraper.

My skin turned gray and white, mottled. Across the dead gray flesh the Etch-A-Sketch lines of feathers were drawn. An eerie design that suddenly was no drawing but three-dimensional reality.

My eyes slid apart, around my head. Eyes that could read a dictionary from a block away. Raptor eyes. Falcon eyes.

My legs shriveled, becoming mere sticks. My

fingers extended out, bare hollow bone that was quickly covered by feathers. Tail feathers erupted from my behind, down my chest, down my back and stomach.

Marco was undergoing a similar mutation. Morphing. It's what we do. It's our weapon.

He was becoming an osprey, I, a peregrine falcon.

Marco began to say something, but his words were cut short as his mouth and nose melted and stiffened and extended into the wicked, curved beak of an osprey.

My talons sprouted, grew curved and sharp.

<I'll meet you there,> I said.

<No, wait.>

<Marco, I'm faster than you are.>

He hesitated. <Yeah. Okay. But Jake?>

<What?!> I snapped.

I expected him to say, "Don't do anything stupid."

<You're not alone, man,> Marco said.

29

CHAPTER 6

Peregrine falcon. The fastest animal on Earth. In a dive I could hit two hundred miles an hour.

But I was a sprinter, not a marathoner. To get to the north end of town I had to soar. Not easy in the evening when the sun has cooled and the concrete no longer steams the air to provide lift for a raptor's wings.

I flew hard, circling for altitude. Marco kept pace at first, but then he fell behind and below.

When you're flying, altitude equals speed. Tobias taught me that. Spend the energy to gain altitude, then you can turn a long trip into a single glide.

I rose and rose, milking every breeze to give

lift to my swept-back wings. Up I went. And at last, boiling with impatience, I made gravity my friend.

I could not see my specific target but I could see the area, the neighborhood. I took aim, whipped my wings, and went into a power glide.

Faster, faster!

The wind tore across my feathers. Around my face. Blearing my eyes. Straining my muscles. One wrong move, one sudden flare of my wings and the speed could snap my shoulders, cripple me, leave me falling, helpless to Earth.

I was a race car driver. One wrong twitch of the wheel and I would spin out of control.

No way to measure my speed, but I was flying faster than I'd ever flown before. The ground raced by. Porch lights and streetlights and bright red taillights were long neon trails.

I was outpacing the cars on the highway below. But I was too low. I'd misjudged the angle. In my haste I'd not gone high enough, and now I was too low, skimming the treetops and peaked roofs and telephone wires, blazing, a rocket!

My muscles burned, my heart was a jackhammer, my lungs burned.

I blew across the mini-mall before I even realized I was there. I braked carefully, took a wide turn, and circled back.

A Starbucks. No. Too public.

A knife shop. Closed. Dark.

Computer Renaissance. Open. Bright. A possibility.

An antique store. Lights on. Half shades drawn up. Two men walking in past a sign that said CLOSED.

I used the last of my speed to buzz the cars in the lot. The lot was full. My dad's car was there.

I landed in the shadows behind the mini-mall. I began to demorph. How to do it? How to attack and get my dad out? What morph, what creature?

My feet sprouted first, pink and bare and huge.

My eyes straddled my bulging, human nose, which had split away from my shrinking beak.

I shot upward as my legs thickened and grew. Hair. Fingers.

My insides gurgled and sloshed sickeningly.

An osprey landed on an overturned crate.

I was fully human. Standing with bare feet on gravel and crumpled cans and scruffy weeds.

I glanced at Marco. He was beginning to demorph.

I began to morph. I felt the powerful, tiger DNA stir in my pulsing blood.

Sharp, gleaming fangs sprouted in my mouth. Claws that could disembowel a bull grew from my fingertips.

<No,> Marco said. <We can't go storming in like the marines, Jake! It's too obvious.>

I was still more human than tiger. The yellow teeth, saber sharp, made speech clumsy. "I'm koink in!"

<Jake, I will have to try and stop you,> Marco said.

We stared at each other for a long, tense moment. A half tiger and a half osprey.

Marco became fully human. I stopped my morph.

"Look," Marco said finally, quietly. "I know you're freaked but if we make this a rescue mission, we're all dead. All of us. Everyone. The Yeerks aren't idiots. They go after your dad and suddenly the Animorphs attack a minor meeting? They can add two plus two, Jake. You let the Yeerks know who you are, Jake, how is that gonna help your father?"

He was right. I knew it but I didn't want to hear it.

"We have to create a distraction. Mess up the meeting but not let them know why," Marco said, as thick, coarse hair began sprouting from his bulging, growing body. "We're gonna buy some time and I've got it all planned. Do your falcon morph again. Your eyes will be better than mine."

"But —" I said.

33

"No buts, Jake," he said. "You know me. You know I've worked it out."

I hesitated, frustrated and not used to being the one taking orders, but I couldn't deny that he was right.

I was losing my clear thinking and that was dangerous.

Surrendering, I concentrated on the falcon morph.

Marco finished his massive, muscled gorilla morph and waited, standing guard until I was done.

<Okay,> I said. <Ticktock, Marco.>

<Well, Rachel's not here so I guess it's up to me,> Marco said, knuckle-galloping his way around to the front of the mini-mall. <Let's do it!>

He stepped out into the parking lot. I flew, watching from above.

My father and my brother were close by. One predator, the other prey. Both, in different ways, in mortal danger.

And if they were to be saved, it was up to Marco. Not me.

CHAPTER 7

It's funny about gorillas. They're gentle creatures by nature. They don't give you the fear chills you get from the big cats or the bears. Mostly when you see them they're zoned out in some zoo cage.

But they are a whole different animal when they're moving. You see a big gorilla moving fast and you get a sense of just how much power you're looking at.

Humanlike? Yes. But like a human who's been built at the Mack truck factory.

Marco walked over to a car.

Grunting, he lifted it up by the rear bumper. Lifted it clear off the ground, back wheels not touching.

And dropped it.

WOOOEEEE! WOOOEEE! WOOOEEE!

I almost laughed. Car alarm!

Marco went to another car. He lifted it. Dropped it. And another. Lift. Drop.

WEEEEYOOOOP! WEEEEYOOOOP! WEEEEY-OOOOP!

HONK! HONK! HONK! HONK!

WaaaaAAAAAAaaaaaAAAAAAaaaaaAAAAA!

The night was filled with clanging, screaming, whooping car alarms.

And then a very familiar car. One we both knew.

Chapman's car. Chapman, our assistant principal. A leader of The Sharing. A Controller.

An enemy.

Marco didn't lift Chapman's car. He punched it. He punched the driver's door with a fist the size of a gallon milk jug.

SHHHLUUUUUEEE! SHHHLUUUUUEEEE!

Then he crashed a huge, hairy gorilla fist down on the hood of my father's new car.

SPREEET! SPREEET! SPREEET!

<Hey!> I hollered, horrified. <That's our car! My dad's going to have a cow.>

<I hope so,> Marco said. Then with barely suppressed glee, <I believe my work here is done.>

He ran back into the shadows. In five minutes he'd be in the air.

It took approximately eight seconds for the doors of the computer store, Starbucks, and the antique store to begin spewing out very angry men and woman.

Chapman came running from the antique store.

So did my father, with Tom close behind.

"What the heck happened?"

"Vandals!"

"Lousy kids!"

"This neighborhood has totally gone to —"

"Call the cops!"

"I'm suing this shopping center!"

"Look at my door!"

That last was Chapman.

The rest of the Controllers from the antique store looked uneasy.

I waited, holding my breath, counting the seconds until my father, followed by a furious, scowling Tom wove through the crowd.

"My car!" my father cried. He practically fell to his knees. "Someone hurt my baby!"

"Mine, too," Chapman said, gazing angrily at the fist-sized dent in his car door. He looked around the street, then nodded at the two big, bulky men who were flanking him.

They split up and started searching the street.

<Chapman's got guys looking for us,> I called to Marco. <Better get out of here.>

37

<Well, come on, dude,> Marco replied. <I'm in a tree down the street. What're you waiting for?>

<I can't go yet, Marco,> I said. <I have to make sure my father's all right. I have to make sure he's still . . . You know.>

I scanned my father's face. Had he become a Controller yet? Stupid. I didn't know. Couldn't know. It's not as if Controllers go around twitching or exchanging Yeerk high fives or playing with their ears. A Controller looks, acts, seems exactly normal.

My father could be my father.

Or he could be screaming, helpless, just beginning to realize that his eyes and ears and mouth no longer belonged to him.

I waited.

And then Tom gave me the clue I was hoping for.

"C'mon, Dad, calm down," he said, going over to him. "We can call and report it when we get home if you want to. Let's go back inside, okay? The meeting just started and a lot of important things are gonna happen tonight. You don't want to miss it. Trust me."

"'Go back inside'?" my father echoed, looking at him like he was insane. "I'm not going back inside! Somebody just tried to break into every

38

car on this street! I'm going home right now and call Joe Johnson!"

"Who?"

"He's our insurance agent, you really should know that, Tom. Come on."

"But, Dad," Tom pleaded, shooting a furious, agitated look back at Chapman, who stood on the curb watching them.

The high wail of distant police sirens split the night.

Chapman shook his head slightly.

"I'm staying till the end of the meeting," Tom said sullenly.

"Then I'll expect you home by ten." My father unlocked the car and got in.

Face tight and twisted with ill-concealed rage, Tom stalked over and stood on the curb next to Chapman, watching as my father drove away.

<He's clean,> I said as an owl landed silently on a nearby ledge. <He's clean. He's okay.>

<Yeah,> Marco said. <Let's get going.>

<Deal,> I said, letting the falcon's keen senses carry me swiftly home.

<Jake? That's round one. You know that,> Marco said, after a moment.

<Yeah,> I said. <I know.>

The fight to save my father had only begun.

39

CHAPTER 8

"I can't believe you took that kind of chance," Rachel said, scowling. "You should have waited for the rest of us!"

It was late that night and we'd all snuck out to meet in Cassie's barn to figure out what to do next.

It wasn't going well.

I was distracted, nervous leaving my father alone in the house with Tom.

Tobias was perched high in the rafters.

Marco was strangely quiet.

Cassie was listening, her face filled with distress.

Ax was watching me with all four eyes.

And Rachel . . .

Well, she was just plain mad.

Apparently Erek had gotten word about our search for my father to Rachel, who'd been shopping at the mall.

She'd rushed to back us up, stowing her packages in a rented locker. In her hurry, she'd forgotten to lock it.

By the time she'd morphed, found Tobias, and flown north, The Sharing meeting had completely closed down. They'd found nothing but cops writing vandalism reports.

When she'd gone back to the locker for her packages, someone had stolen them.

A mad Rachel is a scary thing, and I didn't envy the thief if she ever caught him.

"We weren't looking at a battle, we were just creating a diversion," I said. "Otherwise we'd have waited for you."

I didn't look at Marco as I said it.

<It was an urgent situation,> Ax said calmly.

"Exactly."

Tobias was in the rafters. He ruffled his wings. <A temporary victory. As long as your dad is trying to force Tom to go with you guys, your dad's in danger.>

"I know," I said wearily. "I've thought of trying to convince my dad to lighten up, but there's no way. He's not going to let Tom show disrespect for Grandpa G."

41

"This is so stupid," Rachel said. "I mean, we're suddenly in a knockdown, drag-out fight behind some funeral? This is idiotic! This is a nothing fight. No possible gain for us. All we can do is get hammered."

I nodded. "Believe me, I know, Rachel. It's out of nowhere."

"Had to be *four* days," Marco complained. "Couldn't be two days, which would be no biggie to the Yeerk."

<You will not attend this burial ceremony, Rachel?> Ax asked.

"No, I'm not really related," Rachel said. "Grandpa G was Jake's great-grandfather on his mother's side. We're related on his father's side."

<Ah. And that is important?>

<You know, maybe I'm not getting it, but why didn't Tom just tell your father he's not going and that's the end of it?> Tobias interrupted.

I looked at him.

So did the rest of us.

<What?> he asked, sounding defensive. <I used to do that whenever one of my aunts or uncles wanted me to go somewhere I didn't want to. They never made me go.> He was quiet a moment. Then, abashed, he said, <Oh. Duh. They didn't care what I did.>

"Your relatives are jerks and they didn't deserve you," Rachel snapped.

"My father said we're going as a family," I said. "And knowing my father, Tom would stir up more trouble than he could handle by directly defying him, you know?"

"Sure," Marco agreed. "It's hard to get to those Kandrona rays when you're grounded for life."

"Plus, if he acted really badly, then I'm sure your parents would start looking at him differently," Cassie added. "They might even decide The Sharing is a bad influence and try to make him quit."

I nodded. "Tom's Yeerk is passing as a normal, high-school kid. Bottom line, he can either follow family rules or he loses his cover. The Yeerks have a choice: Keep Tom in place by infesting my father. Or withdraw Tom's Yeerk, put him into a new host, and kill Tom to keep him from talking."

"There's another choice," Rachel said.

"Yeah," I said. I knew. I just couldn't make myself say it out loud.

"What choice?" Cassie asked.

"If the Yeerks can't make his father into a Controller soon enough, they could just kill him. As an orphan Tom's cover isn't affected. Might even be enhanced," Rachel said. And then, looking me straight in the eye, she said, "And Tom would probably be the one to do it."

43

CHAPTER 9

There was only one way to protect my father. Surveillance.

From the moment he left the house for work in the morning until we left for the cabin on Saturday.

Twenty-four-hour surveillance.

I could do most of it. He was my father and although I didn't say it because I didn't want to hurt anyone's feelings, I really didn't think anybody would watch him as carefully as I would.

I did agree to some backup. I knew I couldn't be everywhere at once.

The next morning Tom was all sweet reason and compromise. He went out early, claiming he'd talk to some of the kids from The Sharing before school. See if they'd cover for the commitments he'd made.

Right.

I waited until my father was in the shower, then called myself out of school due to a death in the family.

Luckily, I sound enough like my father.

I went down and lurked in the living room outside the kitchen. I heard the sounds of my father getting ready to leave: slurped coffee, the ritual checking of his beeper, the "Ow!" as he burned his fingers getting an English muffin out of the toaster.

Stupid to morph in the dining room. Idiotic. But I was going to roach morph and I couldn't travel far on those six little legs. Besides, Tom was gone. And my dad wouldn't come this way.

I focused on the roach.

Not my favorite morph. Not anyone's favorite morph. But I needed to be small, fast, and survivable. Maybe a fly would have been better but I'd had a close call as a fly once: Someone swatted me and smeared me all over the storage rack on a plane.

Roaches are harder to kill.

I felt the changes begin. So creepy at the best of times. But standing there in my dining room, shrinking as the chairs grew, shriveling down toward the wood floor you'd gouged with a rake

45

when you were four, falling into the shadow of the table where you ate your Thanksgiving meal . . . that added a level of weird.

I caught unexpected sight of myself in the dining room sideboard mirror. The skin of my face was turning brown, glossy, hard.

I looked away. You don't want to see yourself turning into a cockroach. You don't want to see the way your mouth divides into insect mouth-parts. You don't want to watch your skin melt like wax under a blowtorch and then re-form into a hard, stiff armor. You don't want to be making eye contact with yourself when your eyes stop being eyes and become expressionless black pin-heads.

Maybe you'd think we'd all be used to it. Speaking for myself, at least, no. I'll never be used to it.

Morphing may be a great weapon. It is also a horror beyond imagining.

My bones dissolved. There was a liquid, squishing sound.

A pair of twitching, hairy, jointed roach legs exploded from my swollen insect body like a scene out of an *Alien* movie. I was expecting that. They matched what my arms and legs had become.

Long, feathery antennae sprouted from my forehead.

Crisp, glossy wings cupped my back.

My vision was extremely limited. But my antennae made up for some of that loss. You couldn't call what they did hearing or smell, exactly, more like some weird melding of the two. And yet, not like either.

The plan was for me to hitch a ride with my dad. Tobias would be gaining altitude, looking to hitch an elevator ride on a thermal. From high up he'd be able to watch almost all of my dad's drive from home to his office. Two miles, give or take.

But his reaction time would necessarily be slow. He'd be backup, but if there was an attack it'd be up to me.

I was a roach. I turned like a tiny tank and motored beneath the door.

Whoooom. Whoooom.

My dad's footsteps. Vibration and breeze. My antennae fixed his location. I fought down the roach brain's desire to run.

Whooooom. Whooooom.

Feet the size of an aircraft carrier floated past in the dim distance. No problem. I had roach senses and roach speed married to human intelligence. I was safe.

Safe until I got ready to hitch a ride. My dad wore cuffed pants. The cuff. That would be the place to ride safe and secure.

Just a question of getting there. Up onto the shoe. Up the sock. Should be no problem.

Right.

Light change! Movement! Above me!

I dodged.

BAMMMMM!

CHAPTER 10

It was the size of one of those big oil storage tanks you see on the outskirts of the city. It was ten times my height. A million times my negligible weight. It hit the linoleum floor like a bomb.

Smucker's raspberry preserves.

The jar slammed into the ground an inch from me.

CRASH! The glass shattered.

Huge globs of jam erupted. A glass shard swathed in goo landed like some kind of Nerf meteor beside me. The preserves, a wad twice my own size, hit me in the back as I scurried madly away.

My feet scrabbled insanely. Out of control!

49

The roach brain screaming Run! Run! RunRun-Run! in my head.

The goo fouled my back legs. I couldn't move!

I fought it, but that just made things worse. I lost my balance and rolled over onto my back, all six legs pushing frantically at the raspberry glue. Seeds like footballs jammed the chinks in my armor.

From far, far up in the stratosphere I heard my dad yell a word he's not supposed to use in front of the kids.

Then I guess he saw me. Because he said a worse word.

And I knew right then: He was going to kill me.

The glass shard! It stuck like a boat prow from the goo. I caught the edge with one leg and pushed. Leverage. Something a roach wouldn't understand. But I did.

A second leg grabbed the glass. It would have sliced human flesh, but my hard twig legs weren't hurt.

I pushed and scrambled, shoved, twisted, fighting my way out of the red goo —

WHAM!

The USS *Nimitz* landed on the floor a millimeter from me as I hauled with all my might.

I was on all sixes again, but the goo was all over me, slowing me, dragging at me as —

WHAM!

The USS *Eisenhower* dropped a millimeter ahead of me.

"—— roach!" a booming voice bellowed. "Now I've got jam all over my shoes!"

You're about to have Jake all over your shoes, I thought. I was getting clear of the jam, but it still clung to my spiky legs. I couldn't get traction. I couldn't get up any speed.

WHAM! The *Eisenhower* again.

The wall of shoe sole, twice my own height, appeared in front of me with horrifying suddenness.

I powered my legs and lunged.

I grabbed the sole. I pulled, I powered, I used all the energy that a combination of roach fear and human terror could provide.

Up! I was on the shoe!

"Where'd it go, the lousy . . ."

I tried to get out of sight. I ran for the shadow of the pant leg cuff.

"Aaarrrgghh!" he bellowed in a voice that vibrated every molecule of air in the room.

Now came the dancing portion. My father hopped on one foot, the foot I was on, while attempting to crush me with the other foot.

Not happening. Not now. I had my speed back now. I had the curves and swoops of polished leather, the same color as my own body, to race on.

Running toward the heel, perpendicular to the ground, I hauled. The other shoe poked at me, kicked at me, missed!

At the heel I turned a sharp left and headed vertical. Up the shoe. Over the top onto a soft cotton sock, a sort of gray lawn of scruffy, weirdly twisted grass.

I was in the dark now. Invisible to my father.

"Where'd you go?" he demanded.

Freeze. Just freeze, Jake. Don't move. Don't . . . The preserves were very sweet. Very, *very* sweet, and my roach brain craved sweetness. Sugar. The ultimate lure. And it was still on me. On my legs. On my face.

My mouthparts moved.

I could eat the sugar sweetness off my own leg . . .

"Oh! Oh! Oh!" my dad yelled.

He'd felt me. I'd moved. Now I was in trouble.

WHOMPF!

The dark folds of the sky dropped with sickening suddenness as my dad slapped his leg.

WHOMPF!

WHOMPF!

Don't touch the skin! I ordered myself. If I touched the skin he'd know for sure. He wouldn't stop then.

Had to tough it out. Had to hide. Make him think he was wrong, that he hadn't felt me.

The pants! The gray wool blend that made up the vertical sky. That was the trick.

WHOMPF!

Down it came. I reached, grabbed, and suddenly was lifted away from the sock. I clung to the pants.

The banging stopped. Slowly the pant leg was drawn up. But I was in a fold, invisible.

The pant leg dropped. My dad wiped up the preserves and the broken jar, and drove to work.

CHAPTER 11

The drive was uneventful. I was glad. I couldn't really have taken much more excitement.

Somewhere far above the car Tobias watched. I didn't care. I crept down and out and settled comfortably in the cuff. I was on the left leg so there wasn't much movement.

Ax was waiting at the parking garage by my dad's building. I could feel the car taking tight turns, going up the ramp.

<I believe I see your father, Prince Jake. Are you with him?>

Ax calls me his prince. It's an Andalite respect thing.

<Yeah, Ax. Barely.>

<You have completed two circuits of the open spiral and have ascended.>

That took a couple of seconds. <Oh. Yeah, it's a ramp. The cars use it to get to higher levels.>

<Yes, Prince Jake, it was not overly difficult for me to deduce the purpose of the open spiral structure,> Ax sniffed.

I'm Ax's "prince." But I guess the whole respect thing only goes so far.

We parked. I tensed. Things could get hairy again.

The leg swung out into chillier air and brighter light.

My dad stood up. Stretched. Pulled his medical bag out of the backseat. And we were off to the office.

Swing forward . . . Crunch! . . . Swing back. Swing forward . . . Crunch! . . . Swing back.

<Jake, I'm here,> Tobias reported in. <No sign that anyone followed you.>

<That was quick travel!> I said.

<Soon as I saw you guys leave I headed here. And I was already more than half the way here.>

Somewhere above me, invisible to my roach senses, were a red-tailed hawk and, if Ax had followed the plan, a seagull.

<There is a human watching Jake's father closely,> Ax reported. <He is a large human with more than the typical amount of facial fur. He

appears to be forming facial expressions associated with anger.>

<A ticked-off bearded guy?> Tobias translated. <Can't see him. Must still be under the . . . Okay, I got him. Yeah. He does look ticked off about something. But he's not making any kind of move.>

My dad stopped walking. Wooosh. A door opening. We moved. Closing behind us.

We were in.

As soon as my father stepped into his own office I shot down his leg and hid under the garbage can near his desk.

Waited.

No frantic swiping disturbed the air currents.

Good. Then he hadn't even known I'd hitched a ride.

The floor trembled.

Someone was walking toward my father's office.

"Good morning, Doc. We have a full schedule today. It's ear-infection central out there."

Ten minutes later the first kid came in with his mom.

I spent the day zigging and zagging, zipping along the walls and squeezing into crevices to avoid being seen and squashed.

Every two hours I demorphed and remorphed in the bathroom. The first time it was nerve-wracking. I scrawled a hasty note on a piece of paper towel and stuck it onto the last stall with some used gum.

The note said OUT OF ORDER.

After that I felt a little safer in the out-of-order stall.

It was boring beyond belief. But it gave me a lot of time to think. Too much time.

I'd started out hoping this crisis would give me a way to destroy Tom's Yeerk. Now I was down to hoping I could save my dad from Tom's fate.

I was playing a defensive game. It's easier to attack. On the attack you can pick the time and place. On the defense all you can do is wait. Wait for the enemy to pick his time and his place. And wear out your resources and your people waiting, waiting, knowing all it takes is for the enemy to get lucky and all your tense, cramped-up waiting will be for nothing.

My dad's never been my doctor. I go to one of his partners. You know, it'd be creepy otherwise.

I'd always thought it was pretty cool that he was a doctor. But I guess I hadn't really thought much about it.

On this day, though, there wasn't much else to focus on. So I focused on my dad. Always nice. Always gentle. Joking with the kids and reassuring the moms and dads. Staying calm while the littler kids screamed bloody murder and vibrated the very walls.

He was a good guy, my dad. Not just because he was my dad. Because he was a good person. Because he did his work as well as he knew how and wasn't a jerk to the people around him. That doesn't make you a saint or anything, but I guess when I think about it, that's what I hope I'll do when I'm older: treat my family right, do my job well, not be a jerk to the people I meet. Maybe that's not a huge, ambitious goal, but it would be enough for me. I've done the hero thing. You can have the hero thing. Me, I wanted a day when all I'd have to do was be a decent human being.

It was a long day.

"Good night, everyone," my dad called, finally. "I'll be back Wednesday at the latest. Have a good weekend, Jeannie. You, too, Mary Anne. Stay out of trouble."

A laugh followed us out the door. Now we were moving.

My father was heading out of the office. Back into possible danger.

<Okay, guys, we're moving toward you. We'll be back in the parking deck in a couple of minutes,> I called.

<Hey, Jake?> Tobias said worriedly. <Uh, I don't know if this means anything but the bearded guy is back, hanging around near the elevator.>

<Which floor?> I asked, although I already knew.

The one my father was parked on, of course.

Tobias confirmed it. Ax confirmed it, too.

Hesitate at the door. Then we were outside.

My antennae quivered at the change in the air.

No time to demorph and remorph. If the bearded guy was part of an attack, I was useless.

Nothing but a roach in a cuff.

<Ax?>

<Yes,> Ax said. <I am by your father's vehicle.>

<Is there any place you can morph without being seen?> I asked.

<I have been demorphing behind a large trash receptacle in the alley behind this structure; however, I cannot get back from there to my present position without being seen,> Ax replied. <Should I proceed?>

I didn't know.

If an Andalite suddenly arrived on the scene to save my father, the Yeerks would put two and two together, realize someone close to Tom — like his little brother — knew about his plan, and the Animorphs would be dead.

But in our present morphs, we'd be helpless.

What should I do?

Lose everyone?

Or just my father?

CHAPTER 12

<Prince Jake, do you have any instructions for me?>

<Jake. Make the call, man.>

My family or my friends.

Save one man or save the world.

I was a bug! I couldn't save anyone.

An overt rescue would save my dad and doom us all. Including him.

<What's happening now?> I asked.

<Your father is walking toward his car,> Ax said. <The man with the facial fur is following him.>

<How close?>

<He's about four feet behind your dad,> Tobias said. He was tense. <And closing fast.>

I scampered up and out of the cuff. Onto the

pant leg. Around to the back of the knee. The fabric crinkled with each step. I was horizontal, with the ground on my right. I couldn't see far enough to be sure, but there seemed to be a large, dark wall moving in behind my father. <Am I looking at him?>

<Yes,> Ax said.

Okay. Fine. I might be in a bug's body but I still had a human brain.

I hauled a left and went vertical. Up the pants. Onto the jacket. Up the jacket. Zooming at roach speed along a vertical plane of dry wool fibers.

I came to a stop on the slope of a shoulder. An ear the size of Nantucket loomed above me.

Closer. The dark wall was coming closer. I could almost see a face, a blur, a bristling mass bigger than a rain cloud.

<Jake, what're you doing?> Tobias asked sharply.

<I'm doing what a roach does best,> I said.

<What?>

<Grossing people out and making them say . . .>

I motored. I cranked open the roach's almost useless wings. I flew straight for that beard.

"Aaaahhhhh!" the man yelled.

I landed on his lower lip. The tiny hairs on my legs caught and clung.

He spit. A hurricane explosion of wind!

But I was down on his chin hairs now, walking gingerly from split hair to split hair, like I was tip-toeing across treetops.

"Ugh! Ugh! A beetle!" the man shouted. We began to spin and whirl. He slapped his own face. "Get it off me!"

I zigged left. Then right.

Motored toward his ear. Little roach feet tickled waxy ear skin.

He went wild.

I kept going, on up to his head. Onto thick, matted hair.

"What the heck . . ." I heard my father say in astonishment. "Excuse me, sir, but are you all right?"

Go! I wanted to tell him. *Run, Dad! Run for your life!*

<On our way, Jake!> Tobias yelled.

<NO!> I yelled. <Back off! Back off!>

Suddenly, the air rushed and shimmered with the swoosh of wings.

"Tseeeeeer!" Tobias swooped down, talons extended. I caught an indistinct but terrifying flash of ripping talons.

"Aaaahhh! Aaaahhh!" the man yelled. He was literally beating at his face with one hand to kill me and waving the other in the air to fight off the lunatic hawk and the insane seagull.

Quite suddenly I realized I was no longer on the man. I was on his hair. But I was not on the man anymore.

The hair . . . the toupee . . . was in Tobias's talons being carried off like a doomed mouse.

<I'm going to circle back for —> Tobias began.

<No! No!> I yelled, angry. <We might as well tattoo "The Animorphs were here" on the guy's head! Stay back. Don't attack unless you see the beard move to attack.>

<Oh. Yeah.>

<This is not an attack,> Ax said. <Your father and the man with the facial fur are making mouth-sounds. If this were a Yeerk attack they would not be making mouth-sounds together.>

<Drop the rug,> I instructed Tobias.

He did. The toupee hit the concrete and the man snatched it up and slapped it back on his head. I dropped out before he did and, with Tobias's help, headed in the direction of my dad.

"The bird's gone, the roach is gone, you're okay," my father said soothingly.

"Forget the stupid bug! Forget the stupid, stupid bird!" the man yelled.

He was clearly upset. A hawk had seemingly attempted to grab a cockroach off his head and ended up flying off with his toupee. That's the kind of thing that will put you in a bad mood.

"Is that your car?" the bald man demanded.

"Huh?"

"I said, IS THAT YOUR CAR?!" the man roared.

Like I said, upset.

"Yes," my father said, sounding puzzled. "Why?"

"Because it's parked in *my* spot! MY spot! Mine! I've been waiting to see who keeps taking my spot!"

"How can this be your spot?" my father asked. "There aren't any spots marked 'reserved' here."

"I've been parking in this spot for two years and four months! It's my spot! I don't care how many birds or . . . or my toupee . . . or bugs . . . it's mine!"

<I do not believe this man is a Controller,> Ax said.

<What was your *first* clue, Ax-man?> Tobias said.

<My first clue is the fact that this human is not —>

<It was a rhetorical question,> Tobias said.

<Ah.>

No attack. An argument over a parking space. Funny, really.

Except that I was still left fighting the losing, defensive battle.

Worse, I had frozen. Tobias and Ax had asked for orders and I had frozen. Because I had frozen they'd made the wrong move.

My fault, not theirs. I was in charge, they'd asked me what to do.

I'd hesitated. I'd had no answer. No harm, this time. But if the attack had been real?

I was tired. Ax and Tobias were tired. We were measurably diminished, and the enemy had lost nothing.

The attack was still to come.

CHAPTER 13

I cut Tobias and Ax loose. Told them to get some rest. Tobias objected. He said he'd get the others, they'd mount a surveillance on my house.

I blew him off. Told him to let everyone rest.

Why? I don't know. Maybe I wanted to handle it myself. That way there would be no orders to give. And no second-guessing.

My dad pulled into the garage and I scampered away. I demorphed behind the garage and raced up to my room.

I beat my dad inside. See, I knew his routine. When he comes home he walks down to the curb to check the mail and stands there going through it muttering, "Junk . . . junk . . . okay, magazine . . . junk."

I was in my bed in seconds. Covers up to my chin. Playing sick.

"Jake?"

My door opened. Tom stuck his head into the room.

"What?" I croaked, having a heart failure. I hadn't realized he was home. Had he been home while I'd been demorphing? "When did you get home?"

"What are you doing? Faking sick?"

The Yeerk in his head played the role. Said the words Tom would have said.

I played my role, too. "Yeah. Wanted to stay home and watch Jerry Springer."

"Uh-huh."

"I'm feeling better now, though. I think I'll get up."

He gave me a disgusted look and left. I climbed out of bed and got dressed.

Dinner was chicken soup for me. To "soothe" my upset stomach. My father and brother wolfed down Chinese food.

"What time are we leaving tomorrow?" I asked.

"About nine, so you boys pack tonight and don't forget your suits," my father said, missing Tom's sudden, black scowl. "I talked to your mom. The funeral's on Monday and we'll be leaving for home Tuesday morning."

Tom shoved back his chair. "I'm done," he said, rising and stalking off.

My dad studiously ignored him. "Well, I'm gonna go out and water the lawn one last time before we leave."

"I'll load the dishwasher," I offered, rising.

I rinsed the plates, watching through the window as my father dragged the hose from the backyard to the front.

The house was so quiet. The air so still.

Tom had disappeared into his room.

I pressed my face to the window, leaving a nose smear, and searched the sky until I spotted Tobias gliding high above.

Keeping watch, though I hadn't asked him to.

He looked so free out there.

So calm and confident.

I straightened. Looked around.

And made my decision.

Five minutes, I thought, hurrying up to my room and locking the door behind me. I'll do a five-minute, aerial surveillance. Just enough flying to get hold of myself again. Reassure myself. I'm no good to anybody if I can't think straight.

I stripped down to my bike shorts, opened the window, and concentrated on my peregrine falcon morph.

A lacy pattern rose and spread across my skin, softening into feathers. My fingers melted together to form wing tips as my guts gurgled, slithered, and shifted.

My skull ground and shrunk. My vision sharpened. I zoomed downward, falling, shrinking, wobbling on suddenly skinny, stick legs.

The breeze drifted in the window.

I flapped my wings and hopped up to the sill. Weird. After all this time the idea of jumping out of the second-floor window still bothered me. I was still human, still scared of heights, still not sure my wings would work. I wondered if Tobias ever felt that way.

I spread my wings and took off, swooping down across the backyard, taking care to stay away from Tom's bedroom window.

I caught a slight headwind, just enough to fill my wings, and began to work for altitude.

<Is that you, Jake?> Tobias called cautiously.

<Yeah, I figured I'd join you for a couple of minutes,> I said, leveling off and drifting along on an air current. My falcon eyes could see everything, including a mouse scurrying along the neighbor's fence.

And my dad watering the lawn.

<How's it going?> I asked Tobias.

<I'm getting very little lift in this air,> he complained.

I smiled to myself. A typical Tobias answer.

<How's it going with you?> he asked.

69

<Tense,> I admitted. <It's very tense down there. My dad, Tom, armed camps, man. And me in the middle.>

Tobias didn't say anything. I looked at him. He was higher than me, maybe two hundred yards off.

<Tobias?>

No answer.

<Tobias! What's —>

<Chapman! It *is* him. I couldn't be sure in this light. Six blocks from your house. Him driving, some other guy in the passenger seat.>

I followed the direction of his gaze. A dark car, large, four-door. I focused my gaze. Was the passenger holding something?

<I don't like the feel of this,> I said.

<No,> Tobias agreed.

<My dad —>

<Gun!> Tobias yelled. <The passenger. He's got a gun!>

CHAPTER 14

I was in a stoop before Tobias had finished the sentence.

They were going to pull a drive-by. It was insane. A shooting in broad daylight? Just how important was Tom to the Yeerks? This was reckless!

I was falling . . . no, not falling. I was a rocket on a collision course with Earth. Aimed like a cruise missile for my own house.

The car turned one street closer to mine.

I flared my wings to brake. The hurricane of wind nearly broke them. I strained every muscle, spread every feather. I landed, skidding on the back side of the roof.

No time to demorph inside.

I'd just have to take my chances out here, tucked into the shadowy corner. I began to demorph.

<Jake, what are you doing?> Tobias cried.

I could have answered. I didn't. Tobias knew what I was doing.

<This is stupid, Jake, but I'll cover your butt anyway,> Tobias said. <Don't see anyone watching you. Possible line of sight to the house behind and to the left. There's a little girl near her window.>

My feathers melted. My arms fattened. My beak softened like it was melting. I had to scramble to hold on with talons that were becoming stubby human toes.

<Here comes Chapman,> Tobias reported grimly.

NO!

Demorph! Demorph! Demorph!

Toes . . . hands . . . face . . .

"Aaahhh!" I yelled in surprise.

Suddenly, I was sliding down the steep roof toward the edge.

<Jake! Your brother's right there in the kitchen on the phone!> Tobias shouted. <If you come down on that side, he's gonna see you!>

My fingers scrabbled across the rough shingles for a handhold but it was no use. My fingernails were practically liquid.

I was falling.

Over the edge!

Desperate, I grabbed the sharp, metal gutter.

Dangled. Arms stretched. I tried to haul my legs up, out of view.

<Tom hasn't seen you yet,> Tobias said. <He's got his back to the window. But Chapman is twenty seconds away. It's now or never.>

Tom's voice drifted out through the window.

"Perfect timing," he said coldly. "He's out front alone. Go for it."

I dropped, hit the grass with a dull thud, and gritted my teeth to stay quiet. I crawled past the window, then shot to my feet and tore around the house.

A dark car was turning onto my block. A hundred yards away. Fifty.

"Hey, Dad." I limped over to him, sweating, heart thundering. "Let me do that."

I took the hose.

My dad smiled. "Volunteering, huh? So. What is it you want?"

Twenty yards!

"Just wanted to get outside. Fresh air," I said.

"Unh. Well, thanks, then. I'll go do some packing."

He turned. Too slowly! He walked. Too slowly!

The car was there.

The window was down.

The gunman was staring at my father's back.

I jerked the hose. Water hit the side of the car.

The gunman yanked back in surprise; my father opened the door.

I waved at the car and said, "Sorry!"

The car passed by.

I breathed. My hands were shaking. My heart was a jackhammer.

I pretended to suddenly recognize Mr. Chapman as the car pulled away. "Hey, Mr. Chapman!" I waved.

I felt someone watching me. I spared a quick glance. Tom.

He was framed in our living room window. His eyes burned with rage.

He'd have killed me, too. He would have had my dad gunned down and if I'd gotten in the way . . .

And that wasn't the worst of it. Worse was knowing that my brother Tom, my true brother, had been trapped inside his own mind, trapped watching as the killers prepared to murder his family. Helpless, watching, unable to open his own mouth to shout a warning.

I was clenching the hose so tightly the water was petering out. But I couldn't relax the muscles. Could not.

I don't know how this war will turn out. Don't

know if we'll win or lose or even, somehow, compromise and make peace. But I know one thing: I will kill the Yeerk who has done this to my brother.

I will kill him.

CHAPTER 15

We met in Cassie's barn. All of us but Ax and Rachel. They were watching my house. My dad would be safe with those two.

Tobias calmly, without blame, related what had happened that day and afternoon.

"Stupid," Marco said.

"I can't believe you took a chance like that, Jake!" Cassie said angrily. Cassie doesn't get mad, but she was mad. "Were you *looking* to get shot?!"

"Obviously not," I said, meeting her gaze. "But what else was I supposed to do? Let them kill my father?"

"That's not the point," Marco said, as angry as Cassie, but colder about it. "You demorphed in plain view. And Tobias says it was a matter of a split second whether you ended up machine-gunned on your own lawn."

"The alternative was letting them gun down my father."

"So you figured to let them kill you, too?"

"It worked!" I raged.

Marco threw up his hands in disgust. "Why didn't you have backup? Tobias says you told him and Ax to get lost. And not to get any of us," Marco said. He was leaning back on a bale of hay. Leaning back, but not at all relaxed. "We're supposed to be in this together. If you needed help, you were supposed to ask for it."

"Yeah, I know," I said. "But you guys were in school during the surveillance and tonight, well, I didn't exactly expect Chapman to do a drive-by shooting, you know."

"A mistake on your part," Marco said.

"Yeah. A mistake."

"And today, earlier? Tobias says you froze up when he asked for an order."

"I didn't freeze up, I —"

"We can't afford you freezing up," Marco said.

I glared at him. "You're enjoying this, aren't you? This is payback for when I doubted you over your mother."

"I was ready to do what had to be done," Marco said.

"So am I!"

"No. You're not. You endangered all of us. You demorphed on your roof! On your roof! In daylight. With your brother in the house! If Tom had seen you do that you'd be head down in the Yeerk pool right now, and the rest of us would be standing in line behind you!"

"What's the matter with you all?!" I cried. "That was my father! My father! I'm supposed to just stand by and do nothing?"

Tobias answered before Marco could. <Is it worth exposing ourselves and risking everything, all of mankind . . . literally all the human race . . . just to save one person?> he said quietly. <I'm sorry, Jake. I know he's your father. I know what you're feeling. But it's something we have to think about.>

I looked away. My face was burning. "You know, we talked about this and we decided on surveillance. We watched my father in case he needed protection. Well, he did and I reacted. What did you guys really think I was gonna do?"

"Just what you did," Marco said. "You're too close to this. You can't make this call."

I barked out a laugh. "What, you're going to decide whether my dad lives or dies?" I looked at Cassie.

"Jake . . ." she said.

"You need to back off on this," Marco said

78

quietly. "You can't make this call. Not about your dad and your brother."

"You made it when it was your mom," I said.

Marco shrugged. "Yeah, well, that's me. If it's any comfort to you, I'd like myself more if I was like you. But the question here is, how far do we go to protect your father?" Marco said. "And who is going to make that decision?"

"I'm the leader of this group," I said.

Marco hesitated. He bit his lip. Then, drawing a deep breath, he said, "We need a vote."

"Rachel and Ax aren't here," I said.

<Ax will refuse to vote,> Tobias said. <He'll say it's a human question. He'll say Jake is his prince and he'll do what his prince says. But he won't cast a vote either way.>

"Rachel will back me," I said.

Marco nodded. "Yeah. She will. That leaves it up to Cassie and Tobias."

I didn't look at either of them. I expected to hear Cassie speak up. But she didn't. Silence.

I felt like the ground was falling away beneath me. Cassie doubted me, too? Cassie didn't think I could handle this?

I heard a ruffling of feathers up in the rafters and looked up. Tobias cocked his head, his fierce, hawk's gaze meeting my angry, human one.

I was the first to look away.

Tobias had been there twice when I'd risked

79

my life — and his — to save my father. He knew how important it was to me and he knew how far I'd go to do it.

<You guys are missing a couple of important points,> Tobias said quietly. <First of all, writing off a human life is something the Yeerks would do, not us.>

Cassie nodded. She looked troubled. Like she should have thought of that.

<Second, what if the Yeerks don't *kill* Jake's father? What if they succeed instead in making him a Controller?> Tobias continued. <Jake's already got one Controller in his family; if they make his father one, too, then there's gonna be a couple of very suspicious people watching Jake coming and going all the time, especially when there's Animorph activity. So I don't think it's a question of *should* we save him, but how we do it.>

Thank you, Tobias, I thought silently, staring down at the ground.

<But there's one more thing that nobody's talking about,> Tobias continued, stretching and refolding his wings. <I think we've been on the wrong path all this time. Sitting around waiting for the Yeerks to attack, then saving Jake's father again and again is no plan. The Yeerks may think it was a coincidence at the mini-mall, maybe a coincidence on the lawn, but they can count, you

know? Sooner or later they'll think, "That's too many coincidences.">

"Exactly," Marco said.

<So, why don't we get off the defensive? Do something. Something big that'll distract their attention away from Jake's father until he and Tom and Jake can leave for the cabin tomorrow morning?>

Marco hesitated. He knew the vote had gone against him. At worst he had Cassie on his side. That was two against three, leaving Ax out.

Finally Marco nodded. "Okay, we go on the offensive." He tried a semblance of his usual humor. "I always wanted to die kicking and screaming."

He stepped toward me. He held out his hand. "Nothing personal, Jake. I was just looking out for the group."

I left his hand hanging in midair.

After a while he withdrew it.

"So, what's the plan?" Cassie said, trying to break the hostility of that moment.

"Maybe we could think about —" Marco began.

"I have a plan," I said.

CHAPTER 16

Did I have a plan? Not till that split second. Not till I was face-to-face with Marco and realizing I had to come up with something. Had to.

Sometimes emotion works for you.

We needed a distraction. The distraction I had in mind was big. And would hopefully last until I could get my father out of town.

"Kidnap Chapman," I said.

That made Marco stare. It drew a gasp from Cassie. Tobias laughed like I might be joking. Then he sort of moaned.

Then he laughed again and said, <Well, I'll say one thing: This is going to make Rachel happy.>

A daring plan? Yes.

Crazy? Suicidal? Stupid?

I hoped not.

"Forces the Yeerks to decide their priorities," Marco said. "Do they save Tom or Chapman? Who's more important to them? Chapman. They'll still try and help Tom with his situation, but Chapman disappearing will be a total Red Ball, Maximum Panic situation. It works."

Give Marco credit for one thing: No one is faster or better at seeing the ruthless solution. And Marco is honest.

It wasn't going to be a pretty mission. We didn't have time for subtle.

We hooked up with Rachel and Ax and explained the plan.

Rachel said, "Cool!"

I left Cassie and Tobias to guard my house. I'd have left Marco, too, but he would have taken it as me being afraid to have him around. I wasn't going to give him the satisfaction.

Rachel, Ax, Marco, and I flew to a house across the street and down from Chapman's home on a quiet, suburban street. It was dark. Not late, but dark. I was twenty minutes away from my dad wondering why I wasn't home. Same with the others.

The house was for sale. Vacant. The bushes were overgrown and untended. Perfect for us. Almost roomy at first. Less so as we morphed.

83

"Move over, Marco," Rachel grumbled as his shoulders bulged and muscled up into a gorilla's massive form.

"Oh, come on, you love being close to me," he leered, just before his jaw swung out and his lips became a puffy, black rubber Halloween mask.

I shut my eyes and concentrated on my own morph.

Rhinoceros. For this job we needed blunt, brute force. And nothing is blunter than a rhino.

I heard the thin bone of my human skull crunch and split apart. Heard a sound like grinding teeth as new bone, layers and layers of new bone, filled in the gaps and made an almost impenetrable armor.

My body thickened. My legs, arms, hands, feet, stomach, back, shoulders, all thickened. My skin thickened from human flesh to something resembling a car's leather seat to something as tough and dense and stiff as a saddle.

My ears crawled up the sides of my head.

My eyesight dimmed and blurred.

My neck lost all definition, sucking back into my expanding, blimplike body. Bigger. Bigger.

Huge.

And then, at last, the horn. It grew from my face, down where my nose had once been. Long, curved, dangerous. A primitive, blunt weapon. A horn that could have impaled an armored knight.

But despite the formidable body, the terrifying horn, the power of the rhino, its mind was peaceful, placid. Basically, it just wanted to eat and to be left alone. It was watchful but not scared or angry.

That was okay. I had enough fear and anger for both of us.

"Prince Jake, I am ready. Red-eeee. Eeeee," Ax said. He'd morphed to human, using the DNA combination he'd long ago absorbed from all of us. But he'd stopped the morph partway, distorting his features so Chapman wouldn't be able to recognize him later on.

In his standard human morph, Ax is a strange and beautiful kid. Now, with his eyes a little beadier, his nose stubby and squashed, and his hair darker and shaggier, he bore a startling resemblance to Quasimodo.

Minus the hump, of course.

<Well, Ax, I'll never again think of you as just another pretty face,> Marco said.

<Do you guys see anything suspicious?> I interrupted, twisting my ears around at each new sound and sniffing the air. <I'm half blind with these eyes.>

<Suspicious? Well, I see a bear, a gorilla, a

85

rhino, and some weird kid standing in the bushes, but aside from that, no,> Marco said.

I didn't laugh. I didn't find Marco funny right then. I missed Tobias. We had no one in the air, and we had to cross the street.

<Come on, let's do this,> Rachel said impatiently.

<Ax, move out,> I ordered. <Marco, you, too.>

Ax began to cross the street. It was quiet. I heard bare human feet and bare gorilla feet. I saw shapes, shadows, little else. But I had excellent hearing. I did not hear any approaching cars.

Marco walked as much like a human as he could. A four-hundred-pound human. Once across the street he sidled into the bushes beside the porch. Ax walked up Chapman's porch and knocked on the door.

A wait of several seconds.

The door swung open.

Chapman stood there, holding a newspaper and looking irritated at being interrupted.

"Hello, is Melissa here? Hee-yer? I am a friend of Melissa? I have come here to speak to her regarding a class assignment. Class-uh," Ax said brightly, more or less following the script we'd worked out.

Chapman peered out at Ax and frowned. Sighed. "Wait here. I'll get her."

"Good," Ax said. "She is my close friend and also classmate and thus this is a perfectly normal thing for me to do."

Chapman gave him another look and went to get her.

<Ax,> I whispered. <What do you see?>

<It is as you suspected, Prince Jake,> Ax said. <This Controller has added security devices since our last infiltration. There are motion sensors camouflaged as a mirror frame in the front hallway. And I suspect Dracon beams concealed in the eyes of a statuette facing the doorway.>

<Okay then,> I said as my adrenaline started pumping. <Everyone be ready.>

<I've been ready,> Rachel said grimly.

The front door opened and Melissa stepped out. The door closed behind her.

She looked puzzledly at Ax.

Before she could say anything, two thick, hairy gorilla arms reached up over the railing and lifted her off the steps and down into the bushes.

"Aaahh!" she yelped before a massive hand clapped over her mouth.

Melissa was an innocent. She didn't need to see what was going to happen next.

<Got her tied up!> Marco yelled.

<Go! Go! Go!> I yelled.

CHAPTER 17

<Go! Go! Go!>

I burst from the bushes. Rachel was right beside me, moving in the deceptively fast, rolling gait of the grizzly bear.

Ax leaped from the porch and rolled under cover to demorph.

I crossed the untended lawn, focusing my dim sight on the porch light across the street. But as my massive head swung left and right I lost sight of it. Lights. Everywhere! Which was . . .

<Jake! You're drifting left!> Marco yelled.

I veered. Across the hard concrete of the street. A car! Twin lights raced toward me from my left.

Screeeeeeech!

The driver slammed the brakes. I ignored him. Too late to worry. *Smash and grab and forget subtlety*, I reminded myself.

I stumbled as my thick, tree-trunk legs connected with the porch steps.

<That's it!> Marco yelled.

I barreled, full speed, heedless, horn down for the door.

WHAM-CRUNCH!

The door exploded inward. The frame ripped. Plaster and molding showered.

"HHROOO-UH!" Rachel bellowed, right behind me.

TSEEEEW! TSEEEEW!

Hot, screaming pain. The stench of sizzling hair and flesh.

The Dracon beam in the statuette fired again, burning another black, smoking hole in my armored hide.

It hurt just enough to make me even madder. Now the rhino brain was enraged, too.

I drove forward, through the doorway, slammed into the far wall and knocked the Dracon-concealing statuette over.

Crash!

TSEEEW!

It fired one last, scorching, agonizing beam up into my belly before I crushed it beneath my feet.

Mrs. Chapman ran out from the kitchen.

"Andalites!" she yelled and leveled a hand-held Dracon beam right at my face.

TSEEEEEW!

Searing heat sizzled my forehead, my ear, drilled a burning hole into my very brain, and I staggered, bellowing as the sledgehammer pain rocked me.

The rhino was hurt. Badly.

"GRRROOOWWRRR!" Rachel roared. With a paw the size of a man's head she smacked Mrs. Chapman and sent her flying into the wall. The woman hit, groaned, and slid to the ground, out of the fight.

A flash of blue fur and Ax was with us. <Chapman is escaping up the stairs!>

<Let him go,> I snapped. <We'll even give him a minute to sound the alarm.>

I was reeling. The rhino had taken a head shot. It was dying. The connection between brain and body were fraying.

I counted to ten. <Long enough. Let's go!>

<He's coming out the back window, upstairs,> Marco reported from outside.

<Ax, up the stairs. Rachel, with me.> I crashed toward the living room. The doorway was too narrow. I widened it.

I trampled over the couch and crushed the coffee table like it was made out of toothpicks.

Through the living room. Through the French doors. Literally *through*.

Chapman dropped from down to my right. Marco was there. Reached for Chapman with —

BLAM! BLAM! BLAM!

Chapman fired a handgun. Primitive human technology. Point-blank.

Marco dropped straight back. He hit the ground. Chapman jumped over him.

<Marco!> Rachel yelled.

An Andalite form soared over my head and landed heavily on the grass. Ax had jumped from the second-floor window.

<Rachel, take care of Marco!> I ordered. <Ax! With me!>

Chapman was climbing his back fence. I hit the wood slats and sent him flying. He rolled onto his back and fired.

BLAM! BLAM!

Hammer blows that connected with my throat.

I staggered, plowed into Ax, and knocked him off his feet.

Chapman was up and running through the busted fence.

I was hurt, bleeding, reeling, clinging to consciousness.

And clinging, most of all, to rage. This creep had tried to gun down my father.

I hit him.

He flew, hit the ground, and rolled, groaning. The gun was five feet away.

I backed up a step. Tossed my head. Scented the air and targeted his moaning, prone form.

Die, Yeerk.

I charged.

<No, Jake!> Rachel yelled. <We need him alive! Ax! Stop him!>

I was going to scrape Chapman across the ground. Stomp him, crush him, dig my horn into him.

I saw the horror in his eyes as he realized what I meant to do.

<Prince Jake!> Ax yelled.

I charged. Then, at last, the injuries were too much. As if someone has sliced my legs off, I fell. My momentum carried me, skidding into Chapman.

Chapman tried to rise. Ax nailed him with the side of his tail blade. Chapman went down, unconscious.

I was swirling, swirling down into a black pit. Had to demorph. Demorph. It was dark . . . dark enough that Marco couldn't say . . .

Marco. Had I gotten him killed?

Melissa must have worked the gag out of her mouth. "Mommy? Daddy, where are you?!" Melissa Chapman wailed.

CHAPTER 18

I demorphed to the sound of Melissa's terrified cries and the wail of approaching police sirens.

I stood up, frazzled, confused. Rachel was there, human. Ax was gone. Marco . . .

Marco reached down and lifted Chapman easily up onto his shoulder.

"You okay?" I asked him.

<Demorphed, remorphed, good as new,> he said tersely. <Let's move out. With your permission, mighty leader.>

We moved. Rachel and me providing what limited visual cover we could for Marco. We ran across the street and down. Back to the vacant "For Sale" house.

We were going to keep Chapman a prisoner right where no one would ever suspect: Within two hundred yards of his own home.

Ax had disconnected the burglar alarm when we got there. The back door was open.

We hustled inside. Marco dropped Chapman unceremoniously in the empty, wood-floored living room. Then he popped his fist through the glass of a door connecting dining room and living room. The glass fell toward Chapman.

With his weak but nimble Andalite fingers Ax tied a rag over Chapman's eyes. Ropes went around his wrists and ankles.

We stood there, looking down at him. He was in our power. For now.

"I wonder —" Rachel started to say.

I shook my head and put my finger to my lips. He couldn't be allowed to hear human voices.

<He is still unconscious,> Ax said.

Marco reached down and poked Chapman in the ribs with a finger like a bratwurst. The Controller did not react.

I went to the kitchen. I found an empty coffee can someone had used to store nuts and bolts. I filled it with cold water, returned to the living room, and poured it on Chapman's face.

He sputtered and cursed.

Then he tried to move his hands.

<Okay, Ax, it's all yours,> Marco said, stepping back.

Rachel and I remained silent.

Ax moved forward, hooves clopping on the bare, wooden floors, circling Chapman on purpose, letting him hear that his interrogator was an Andalite.

<So, Yeerk,> he sneered imperiously. <Now you are mine.>

Chapman started to tremble.

He whimpered, soft and low.

I didn't look at Rachel; she didn't look at me. Neither of us was thrilled about this. We had to make Chapman think he was being interrogated by an Andalite warrior.

We had to make him think he would be tortured. Moments earlier I would have killed him. Even now, I felt no pity for him. But that didn't change the fact that we were trying to terrify another living, sentient creature.

If you're the kind of person who gets off on that, you need help. I was asking a lot of Ax. Too much.

But he was determined to play the role.

<If you want to live — and I need not remind you that is in my power to end your life right now — you will answer my questions,> Ax said with exaggerated Andalite arrogance. <What is the extent of the Yeerk penetration of Earth?>

Chapman shuddered but stayed silent.

<Do not defy me, Yeerk filth!> Ax roared. <Name all the Yeerks in positions of power!!>

No answer.

<I will keep you here, you know,> Ax said, changing tactics and using a silken, deadly thought-speak voice. <Kandrona starvation, Yeerk. It is a terrible way to die. How long since you visited the Yeerk pool? How many days, how many hours do you have before the terrible need begins to —>

I'd seen and heard enough. I jerked my head toward the door. Rachel and Marco followed me. Marco demorphed as he went.

Ax's words had conjured up a dark, miserable picture in my mind.

The death he had falsely promised Chapman was the one my brother Tom was going to suffer, because the Yeerk in his head would be cut off from Kandrona rays.

"Jake?" Rachel whispered, once we were outside.

I shook my head. Couldn't answer.

I headed for home past the crowd of neighbors and cops and emergency vehicles that had clustered around the Chapman home.

So far, the plan had worked.

Ax would continue to interrogate Chapman.

Maybe get rough with him.

This was what I'd led us to. Marco nearly killed. Melissa Chapman terrorized. And Ax left to spin tales of horror for a helpless captive.

Marco wouldn't need to take another vote: I was done being the leader.

CHAPTER 19

I lay awake all night.

Tense.

Listening.

Listening to the sounds coming out of the darkness.

Waiting for Tobias, who had settled down two hours ago in the tree outside my window, to suddenly shout, <The Yeerks are coming, Jake!>

It didn't happen.

At 3:30, I slid out of bed, careful not to step on the creaky part of the floor, and tiptoed into the hallway.

My father's door was half-closed.

I peeked in.

He was sleeping, the moonlight shining on his face.

I inched further down the hall.

Tom's door was closed.

I held my breath and pressed my ear to the door.

Nothing.

Palms sweating, I gripped the knob and without wiggling it, slooooowly cracked open the door.

Tom's bed was empty.

I shivered.

Closed the door and hurried back to my own room.

My brother was gone.

Probably out with the rest of the Controllers, searching frantically for Chapman. Tobias must have seen him go but didn't want to wake me up.

I climbed back into bed and lay there, wide-eyed and listening to the house settling.

Wondering what my brother was doing. How he was feeling.

And imagining how frantically the Yeerks were searching for Chapman.

How scared and desperate Tom's Yeerk must be by now, knowing he was suddenly just priority number two.

"Are you scared, Yeerk?" I whispered into the darkness.

I thought about how I'd feel if my friends left me to the Yeerks to save someone more important.

Not a good feeling.

And what about the real Tom inside?

What was he thinking?

I didn't know and I couldn't stand the thought, but I couldn't stop thinking about it.

Couldn't let it go.

I was the leader.

I should have been able to come up with a better, surer plan.

If I couldn't figure out a way to save my own family, then how could the other Animorphs rely on me, anyway?

How could I rely on myself?

My numb, foggy brain begged for sleep but it wasn't happening.

The hours crept by.

<Hey, Jake, are you up? Are you awake? If not, wake up. Your brother just snuck in through the back door,> Tobias said as the sun rose and my bedroom was filled with brilliant, golden sunlight.

I couldn't answer. Wasn't anything to say anyway.

I heard Tom creep past my room. Heard him open, then close his bedroom door.

I swung wearily out of bed and opened my window.

Time to go check on Chapman.

CHAPTER 20

I used my peregrine falcon morph and flew to the empty house where Chapman was being held hostage.

I was tempted to continue holding Chapman and starve his Yeerk to death. Let the Yeerk Empire know that they were vulnerable, too. That we could be cruel enough to kill, when pushed far enough.

The sick, dark anger inside of me wanted to. And had nearly tried, last night in rhino morph.

I landed in a tree near the window.

Ax was still inside.

<Everything going okay, Ax?> I asked from outside the house.

<Yes, Prince Jake,> Ax replied. <I was careful

to walk directly over the glass from the broken window, making it crunch very loudly. I believe this Controller will use the glass to sever his bonds once I have left.>

<Good,> I said.

<No, Prince Jake, nothing about this is good,> Ax snapped. <This is not behavior suitable to a warrior. I will not do this again.>

<Understood, Ax,> I said.

<The human daughter of this Controller has walked through the neighborhood crying for her father. I have heard her. As I have heard the terror of this Controller. I will gladly fight this Controller and even, in fair battle, kill him, but I am not a torturer.>

I'd never heard Ax this mad. Never even close.

<It's my fault, Ax. My responsibility. You only did what I asked you to do, as your prince. This is on me.>

<No. My actions are my actions and are my responsibility,> he said, but his anger had softened a little. <I am sorry to have expressed anger.>

<Ax-man, you are entitled,> I said wearily.

He didn't say anything for a while, and I sat, miserable and ashamed, in the tree.

<I must play out the charade,> Ax said wearily.

<Yeah.>

I sat there, fluffing my feathers against the morning chill, watching as the first early commuters headed for their cars, slung their briefcases and laptops in the backseat, and headed off for work. Normal. A normal day in a normal American suburb.

Except that across the street a girl cried for a father she'd long ago lost without knowing it, and here, a creature part man and part Yeerk was threatened with painful death.

<Kandrona starvation, Yeerk. That is what awaits you. The slow weakening . . . the growing madness . . . the terror as you begin to realize that nothing, nothing can save you. Is that what you want? Help me, Yeerk. Help me help you.> Ax could have used private thought-speak, thought-speak only Chapman would hear. But he wanted me to hear.

<Your last chance. I will leave you here, bound, helpless, the thirst and hunger of your human host body adding to your own desperate need.>

If Chapman answered I didn't hear him. I guess he did answer, though, because Ax said, <Your choice, Yeerk.>

Moments later Ax was morphed to osprey and soaring away from the house.

Chapman would escape. We had left the broken glass there deliberately. Chapman believed we were all Andalites. He would think we were too unfamiliar with the human world to know that glass can cut.

<And he will return to his people a hero,> Ax said. <This will become an oft-repeated and much celebrated chapter in Yeerk history. My name will become legend, synonymous with ineptitude. A brutal fool of an Andalite.>

<Ax, I wouldn't have asked you to do it if it wasn't so important.>

Ax looked at me, fierce hawk eyes glittering. <Important to you, Jake, or to the war effort?>

I didn't answer him.

I wanted to believe it was important to both, but my weary brain couldn't even form the words to convince myself, much less him.

Ax flew back to his woods, muttering something about cleansing rituals.

I flew home and relieved Tobias.

<Everything looks cool, Big Jake,> Tobias said. <So, what's the plan? How do we follow you guys up to the mountains?>

<We leave at noon. We were supposed to leave earlier, but my dad has some stuff to do this morning. I'll meet you all at Cassie's barn at nine to set the plans.>

<Okay. Later.>

Tobias flew off.

We were leaving for Grandpa G's cabin in two hours. By the time the others realized I wasn't going to meet them at the barn we'd be long gone.

I was done using my friends on this mission. I was tired of Marco's doubts and Ax's honor and even Cassie's wary sympathy.

This was my family. My brother, the killer. My father, the target. And me, the fool in the middle.

Just the three of us.

If my brother Tom, in a desperate, last-ditch attempt to save himself, tried to kill my father, then I would morph.

And the last thing my brother would see was me, his brother, his unknown enemy, rear up and destroy him with all the ruthless, savage power that was mine to command.

I had told myself that I would do whatever had to be done, and I would.

Suddenly, I needed to talk to Cassie. And maybe, when it was all over, I would.

CHAPTER 21

Homer had already been taken to Rachel's, where he'd spend the next four days being petted and pampered and played with.

Too bad he and I couldn't have changed places.

And now my father, Tom, and I had eight hours of boring, highway driving ahead of us.

Tom sat in the front with my father, sulking and giving monosyllabic answers to my father's forcedly cheerful questions.

I answered a few, but my heart wasn't in it either, and after about ten miles, my father just stopped trying.

I sat tensely in the back, watching Tom, searching for any signs of Kandrona withdrawal.

Nothing.

Maybe he'd fed last night, in between searching for Chapman.

It wouldn't matter though, because we still wouldn't be home before the three-day limit.

I tried to imagine life without Tom. Without my older brother. I'd be an only child. Marco was an only child. So were Cassie and Tobias.

But I wasn't and I didn't want to be. Saving Tom was the reason I'd agreed to be an Animorph. I hadn't wanted it, any of it. But then I'd learned the Yeerks had taken Tom and made him one of their own.

It was for him that I had endured that first horrifying morph. It was to save him that I had gone down into the Yeerk pool, that unsuspected house of horrors.

I wasn't going to lose Tom to the Yeerks. I had to keep that hope alive.

But I had to keep my father alive, too. The Yeerk in Tom's head was locked in battle with me, though he didn't know it. We were deadly enemies on a field of battle where two innocent people, my brother and my father, stood directly in our line of fire.

After an hour or two, I fell asleep.

Woke up four hours later as we pulled into a rest stop.

We used the bathroom. Wolfed down luke-warm hamburgers and stiff, cardboard fries.

Headed back out on the road.

Finally, when I was numb with nerves and cramped from sitting, my father turned the car down a hidden, gravel road.

"We're almost there," he said tiredly.

I sat up.

So did Tom.

Thick forest lined the road, the tree branches seeming to reach for the car. The air was cooler, cleaner, and smelled of dark, moist dirt.

A mouse scurried out onto the road in front of us. Sat up, unafraid, and watched as we slowly approached.

"Tseeeer!" A hawk swept down out of nowhere and seized it. Carried it off.

"Survival of the fittest," Tom murmured, his mouth curving into a small, secret smile.

I looked at the side of his head. I looked at his ear, wanting to picture the foul, gray slug that was inside his brain.

Do you have a plan, Yeerk? Are the woods full of your allies? Do the Hork-Bajir lie in wait? Do the Bug fighters hover above us, waiting for the signal?

Or, like me, are you planning on handling this by yourself?

Don't take me on by yourself, Yeerk. You won't win.

Survival of the fittest, Yeerk.

"Finally," my father said, sighing and parking the car. "Everybody out."

My boots crunched noisily on gravel and pine needles. The sound of car doors slamming was both loud and insignificant in the quiet of the woods.

Grandpa G's cabin sat in the middle of a small, grassy clearing surrounded by dark, towering pine trees. There was a well-worn path leading from the front door straight down to the dock at the lake.

Silence. Then, my mother and my grandparents spilled out of the cabin. We were hugged and fussed over, fed and herded back out to the porch to relax.

"It makes me sad to think that Grandpa G isn't here anymore," my mother said quietly, watching as the sun set over the lake. "He really loved this place."

"I remember when he came home from the war," my grandfather mused. "He was a different man. He said he wanted nothing but peace after seeing so much."

"Some people just can't deal with the reality of war, I guess," Tom said offhandedly, earning shocked looks from my parents and grandparents.

"And what would you know about war, Tom?" my grandfather said levelly, like he was trying not to sound as angry as he felt. "I don't recall hearing about your enlistment."

"You're right," Tom said quickly. "That was a stupid thing to say. I guess I was just thinking about Grandpa G spending all his time out here, alone."

Everybody relaxed and went on reminiscing.

But I didn't. I just sat and watched and listened.

I had no plan. No plan but to react when Tom struck. I was waiting, playing defense again.

Your move, Yeerk.

CHAPTER 22

"Why couldn't they have the funeral tomorrow?" Tom said later that night, once we were in the attic bedroom. "I mean, Sunday or Monday, what's the difference?"

"Grandpa G wanted it that way," I answered, looking around the small, dark room. "And besides, Mom said they never bury people on Sunday around here. Sunday is for the wake, Monday for the burial."

"Yeah, well, it's stupid," Tom said, watching me crouch in front of an old chest. "What're you doing?"

"Nothing," I said, lifting a stack of old, dusty books off a small, dark gray leather trunk. "Don't you remember this, Tom? This is Grandpa G's old footlocker."

Tom glanced at it. Then he looked past it, around the room, searching for something to do.

I opened the footlocker, filled with sudden urgency. "Remember back, like, I don't know, when I was ten or so? He showed us his canteen and these pictures of his outfit from the Battle of the Bulge?"

"Maybe," Tom muttered.

"They didn't know whether they were gonna freeze or starve or get shot. That's what he said."

Tom rolled his eyes. Indifferent. *Perfectly Tom,* I thought, almost admiring. The Yeerk was keeping up the illusion. Playing the part to perfection.

"Christmas, when they were all homesick in their foxholes, they sang 'Silent Night.' The enemy sang it, too, in German. Far off they heard it. Both sides lonely for their homes. Both sides wishing the war was over."

"Uh-huh."

"Don't you remember how he told us all this, Tom?" I pressed, wanting him to admit he remembered. Wanting, ridiculously, the real Tom inside to push hard enough to break through, just for a minute, and be my totally human brother again.

Tom sighed. "Vaguely. I'm not real big on old war stories."

I lifted out the small box that held Grandpa G's Silver Star and his Purple Heart. "He was a brave guy. He believed in honor. All that stuff out of old movies. Honor and courage and all."

"Yeah, well, that was all a million years ago," Tom said. "Honor and courage aren't what matters, not in the real world. What matters is whether you win. After you win then you start talking about honor and courage. When you're in battle you do whatever you have to do. Honor and courage and all that? Those are the words you say after you've destroyed all your enemies and anyone else who gets in the way."

"You're wrong," I said flatly.

He rolled his eyes, bored now. "You're a kid." I saw Tom's eyes narrow. "What's this?" He reached into the footlocker and lifted out a cracked leather scabbard. From the sheath he drew a dagger. The blade glittered dully in the dim lamplight. It was a long blade, maybe eight inches or so.

Suddenly, the attic was close and airless.

"SS," Tom mused, examining it. "It's an old Nazi dagger. Grandpa G must have taken it off a dead soldier as a souvenir. Cool."

"What're you gonna do with it?" I asked.

Tom cocked his head and looked at me.

"I mean, you can't take it," I added hurriedly. "It isn't yours."

"Hey, you get the medals, I get the dagger, right?" he said. "It's perfect. You can sit around thinking about honor and bravery and all, and I get the weapon that gets the job done. Sounds fair to me."

I kept my expression as blank as I could. I, too, was playing a part.

"I'm not taking anything until I talk to Mom and Grandma," I said, carefully putting the medals back in the velvet case and waiting for Tom to do the same with the dagger.

"Well?" I said. "Come on, man, put it back."

"Mom and Grandma," he mocked. "You're still such a kid. You think everything is so simple, don't you? That it's all either right or wrong, black or white. A good guy, a bad guy, and nothing in between."

No, Yeerk, I don't. Not anymore. I used to. But I've been across the line; I've done things I can't let myself think about. I know all about the shades of gray.

I said, "Sometimes even the good guys do bad things. Doesn't mean there's no difference between good and evil."

"Good and evil," he said with a tired smile.

"Strong and weak. That's the reality. Winners and losers."

"The knife, Tom," I said.

He laid it back in the footlocker.

He turned out the light. We crawled into our respective bunks. Our separate foxholes.

CHAPTER 23

I was cold.

Freezing.

Night.

My feet were solid blocks of ice despite the filthy rags I'd wrapped around my torn boots. My fingers were numb, stiffly clutching my M-1 rifle.

I had a clip and a half of ammo. One grenade. If the Germans came it would be over fast.

I hadn't had a warm meal since . . . Had I ever had a warm meal? Had I ever, ever been warm? Hadn't I always been in this freezing foxhole, this black hole punched in the snow? Hadn't I lived my entire life right here at the edge of the dark forest, shivering, shaking, waiting to hear the scream of incoming shells, waiting to hear the clank-clank-clank of the tanks?

Christmas Eve.

Merry Christmas.

I heard a racking cough from the next foxhole. Matthews. He was from Arkansas. Alabama. One of those places. A southern boy. A kid, one of the last replacements to make it to our unit.

"Hey, kid," I said in a hoarse whisper. "Goose or ham?"

"What?" he gasped between coughs.

"Back home, what does your mom cook for Christmas dinner? Goose or ham?"

For a while he didn't answer. Then, "Ham."

"Yeah? We always have a goose. My mother cooks up a goose."

From a second foxhole, to my right, a voice said, "Don't listen to him, kid. Sarge ain't got no mother."

I think the kid laughed. Hard to tell with the coughing. Pneumonia, most likely. He should be evacuated. But no one was being evacuated. The joke was that even getting yourself killed only got you a three-day pass and then it was back to the line.

"Sarge," he called when the coughing subsided. "Sarge."

"Yeah."

"You write the letter, okay? I know it's the

captain's job, but he don't know me. You write the letter."

There was only one letter. The one that would inform Private Matthews's family that he was among the honored dead.

I said something rude and obscene. Couldn't have him thinking that way. You start thinking you'll die, maybe you do.

"Tell my mom I did okay," he said.

"Tell her yourself, I'm not the U.S. Mail," I said. "You tell her when you get home."

"Merry Christmas," a bitter voice on my right said.

For a while no one spoke. We listened for the incoming shells. We listened for the tanks. We waited for the crack of a sniper's rifle and the cry of a man dying.

But then the thin, biting air was filled with the sound of voices, ragged at first and then soaring into a harmony that sweetened the night, bringing me home to my family, filling my empty, aching belly and soothing my torn, battered heart.

"'Silent Night.'"

"'Holy night,'" Private Matthews whispered, smiling.

"I think I hear the Germans singing, too," I said.

"Yeerks don't sing," Matthews said. Suddenly, he was beside me.

He opened his eyes. Bared his teeth.

And rammed the Nazi dagger straight into my heart.

My eyes snapped open.

Darkness.

I sat up, heart pounding.

Glanced sideways.

The other bed was empty.

I was at Grandpa G's cabin.

Sharing the attic bedroom with my brother.

And it was late. Too late for Tom to be up.

My breath froze in my throat. I rolled over and opened the footlocker.

The dagger was gone.

CHAPTER 24

I shot out of bed.

Pulled on sweats and padded out of the bed-room.

Down the stairs.

The night-light cast a thin, golden glow.

Snoring. Murmuring.

Everyone was still sleeping.

I paused in the main room and looked at the pull-out couch.

My mother was in it.

My father was gone.

Oh, no! Was I too late? Had I given Tom the exact and perfect chance he'd been waiting for?

I eased open the front door.

Creeee . . .

I went still.

Held my breath.

Nothing.

Squeezed out through the gap and waited in the shadows on the porch.

Listened.

The breeze carried the sound of voices.

There!

My father and Tom were sitting down at the end of the dock, talking and dangling their feet in the water.

My father laughed and gave Tom's shoulders a quick, spontaneous hug.

Tom's sweatshirt bunched up in the back.

Revealing, for a moment, the gleaming dagger wedged in his pocket.

My father didn't notice it. He laughed again and removed his arm.

Tom and my father, sharing a private conversation in the middle of the night.

Tom, the betrayer.

My father, the betrayed.

I had no doubt who'd instigated it.

Tom, apologizing for his bad behavior. Wanting to talk to my father, man to man.

Lying.

He'd lured my father outside, where no one would hear.

Tom slipped his hand behind him and closed his fingers over the dagger.

Tightened his grip on the handle.

I had to do something.

Fast!

I edged off the porch and took off running, keeping to the deep, dark tree line and morphing as I went.

I didn't care that once I did, Tom would realize I was the enemy.

And that once he knew, I couldn't let him live.

His action, my reaction.

Adrenaline pulsed through my veins.

Drowned out the fluttering panic.

Thick, orange-and-black fur sprouted, rippling over my body. My nose flattened, widened. My senses lit up. Smell! Hearing! Night vision almost as good as an owl's.

I could smell my brother's exultation.

He was excited, anticipating the kill.

Tiger senses. Tiger strength. Tom would be helpless. A boy with a knife against a tiger? Like going up against a tank with a Nerf gun.

I fell forward as my bones ground and remolded into four strong, muscular legs.

Hurry! I shouted silently, stumbling as my feet widened and my toenails curved into deadly claws.

But I was still only halfway to the dock when Tom withdrew the glittering dagger.

CHAPTER 25

CCCRRRRAAAACCCKKKK!

The sharp sound split the night.

My father and Tom looked up in shock as the wooden dock tilted and collapsed with a screech.

They scrabbled to hold on, but the planks were an accordion being squeezed. The entire dock was being folded back on itself by some massive force.

Tom and my father both slipped into the water.

"Hey!" my father shouted, going under.

He bobbed back up, gasped, thrashed, and went down again.

I stopped dead in the shadows, surprised, amazed, waiting to see what was happening.

124

My dad could swim like a fish. Why was he surfacing and going back under?

"Glug," he croaked, surfacing several yards away from the ruined dock and almost immediately disappearing again.

It was almost as if something was pulling him down and towing him away from Tom. . . .

Tom was frantic, splashing and swinging around in the water, not trying to save my father, just trying to keep him in sight. Why? So he could watch him die? So he could catch up with him and use the dagger?

Silent anger roared in my ears.

My fur rippled and stood on end.

My still-human mouth tightened into a snarl.

I moved forward again.

"Gak," my father burbled, surfacing another ten yards away from the dock.

Tom swung around in the water, searching for him.

Suddenly, a fin broke the lake's surface behind Tom.

Shark? I thought blankly. *Shark in a mountain lake?*

No, not a shark.

A dolphin!

Before I could move, the fin sliced through the water and something slammed straight into Tom's back.

"Oof!" Tom arched, eyes wide with surprise, and shot forward, plowing facedown in the rippling lake.

He didn't move after that.

The fin — no, there were more than one — the fins slipped soundlessly below the surface.

"Tom! Tom, are you all right?!" my father yelled, clambering up onto shore. He'd been dragged some twenty yards down the lake and was staggering back through the thick, vine-covered underbrush.

Tom was floating facedown, motionless in the water.

My father would never get there in time to save him.

I could. The tiger can swim. I could save him.

But I didn't move. Frozen. Brain locked around the simple fact that if Tom died he would, at last, be free. That if the Yeerk died I would have had my revenge. That we would be safer, stronger, freer with the Controller named Tom dead and gone.

Didn't know what to do.

<Jake! Demorph!> a voice ordered. <You're in the open. Demorph!>

I obeyed, glad for once to take orders rather than give them. Relieved to have the decision made for me.

The others had followed me to the cabin.

126

They'd backed me up even though I'd said not to. They'd taken the decision out of my hands.

I stepped forward. My feet had remolded to human.

I stood up. My fur had disappeared.

Tom would drown unless I saved him.

Saving him might still mean my father's death.

Help me! I wanted to scream. *Tell me what to do!*

The lake water rippled. Surged.

And suddenly Tom's limp, unconscious body was skimming across the water like a surfboard, being pushed rapidly toward shore.

I ran to the water's edge. My reflection in the moonlit ripples was human.

Panting, I dragged Tom's body up onto the land.

Flipped him over.

Water streamed from his still face.

His right leg flopped and twisted at a crazy, sickening, unnatural angle.

"Help," I croaked, leaping to my feet. "*Help!*"

Tom groaned. Coughed.

He gagged and barfed up buckets of smelly lake water.

"Don't move," I babbled, trying to hold him still as he thrashed. Something was wrong with

127

his leg. There was a hinge where there shouldn't be one. "I think your leg is broken."

"Jake!" my father shouted, staggering up. His clothes were sagging, sopping, and ripped, and he was covered with dark, slimy mud. "Is Tom all right?"

"No," I said, shaking my head. "Someone better call an ambulance. Dad, hurry!"

My father ran to the cabin.

I looked down at Tom. Inside his head was a killer. He'd almost killed my father.

But what I saw, the eyes I looked into, those belonged to my big brother.

I settled into the mud next to him.

His face was white and tight with shock, his eyes filled with dark agony. His teeth were chattering and tears leaked down into his hair.

"Get out of here, midget," he gasped, writhing. "Get out of here and leave me alone!"

"No," I said, moving closer. "I . . . don't think so."

And I didn't until I heard a deep, pulsing THWOK THWOK THWOK and a medevac helicopter dropped out of the starry sky and swept Tom away.

CHAPTER 26

"Okay, honey. You, too."

My father hung up the phone and sighed. He ran a hand through his rumpled hair, then turned to face the sea of anxious faces.

"Well?" I asked.

"Your mom says they medevaced Tom all the way back to the hospital back home," my father said, plopping down in a chair. "It seems he has a complex break and our hospital's the only one in the area equipped to deal with it."

"No kidding," I said, not at all surprised.

Of course: back home. Back where there were plenty of Controllers around to make absolutely certain Tom would have access to the Yeerk pool's lifesaving Kandrona rays.

"He's in some pain and he'll be laid up for a while, but at least he's gonna be okay," my father said thickly. He reached over and hugged me. "Thank God you got there in time to save him, Jake."

"I didn't save him," I said. "He drifted into shore. I just grabbed him and hauled him out of the water."

"And saved him," my father insisted, releasing me. "I was really scared tonight, Jake. I don't ever want to lose either one of you."

"Me, either," I said.

And we had come so close. A dagger half-drawn. A tiger running.

"Well, I need a cup of coffee," my father said.

"I'll make it," my grandmother said.

"Make one for me, too, please," my grandfather called after her.

"First thing tomorrow morning, I'm gonna call whoever built that dock and read them the riot act," my father said. "And then I want to talk to somebody about the undertow or the current or whatever it was that dragged me down that lake. It's dangerous!"

"Yeah. Um, look, I'll be right back, okay?" I said. "Need some fresh air." I slipped out of the door and into the fading darkness.

I stood for a moment listening, but it was no use.

Human hearing is so limited.

I spread my hands like, *Well?*

<Over here, Jake,> Tobias called from a thick stand of pine trees.

I walked over and met them in the shadows.

Without my asking, they told me how they'd done it.

How Tobias had kept endless watch and sounded the alarm when Tom and my father exited the cabin.

How Cassie had quickly morphed to whale and struggled through a shallow, nerve-wracking twenty feet of water to ram the dock, praying she wouldn't be beached before she got there.

How Rachel and Ax had morphed into dolphins, rammed Tom, broken his leg, and dragged my father to safety.

I wanted to say a lot.

Like how they'd saved my family.

My sanity.

"Thanks," I said.

"Hey, don't mention it," Rachel said fliply. "We needed a vacation, anyway."

<We have spent time exploring that decrepit, architectural structure riddled with rodents and assorted wildlife,> Ax said, turning an eye stalk toward the abandoned hunting lodge across the lake. <We discovered several extremely large spiders.>

"And rats. Don't leave out the rats," Cassie said with a laugh.

<Personally, I had fun,> Tobias offered.

"That's because you got to eat like a pig," Rachel said.

They were trying too hard.

"Where's Marco?" I said.

Cassie shrugged. "He didn't know if you'd want to see him right away. Thought you might need some time to calm down or whatever."

"Come on out, Marco."

He stepped into view from behind a tree. He looked a little leery. Which, given the way I'd treated him was not surprising.

"Hey, Big Jake."

"Marco. This had to be your plan."

"Pretty much."

"Yeah. Well. Good plan."

"Thanks. Couldn't have done it without the Chee," Marco said, shrugging like it was nothing. "They're the ones who piloted the medevac helicopter and insisted on taking Tom back home. Without them, all we would have had was a kid with a busted leg out in the middle of the woods."

"Tom's back home. Alive. My dad's alive. Crisis past. I should have thought of it myself. Tom, injured, had the perfect excuse for not coming on this trip. I should have seen that."

Marco shrugged. "Yeah, well . . ."

"I was too close to it," I said. "You were right. I was too close to see things clearly."

Marco didn't argue. He didn't gloat, either. I guess we each have our strengths and weaknesses. Marco's strength is the ability to see the way to the goal, even when it means disregarding consequences and feelings and basic right and wrong.

He'd seen this solution when I missed it.

I took Marco's arm and drew him away from the others. To where they wouldn't hear.

"You're my best friend, Marco. If you ever again tell me I'm losing it, getting too involved, can't lead —"

"You'll kick my butt?" he interrupted with a grin.

"No. I'll listen. I'll listen. Then I'll kick your butt."

He laughed. I laughed. What can I say? Marco and I have been friends forever.

We started to rejoin the others. I stopped him. "Marco?"

"What?"

"This whole plan worked because Tom came outside and made himself vulnerable. What would have happened if he hadn't?"

Marco didn't look at me.

"You had to keep me from blowing it at all

133

costs," I pressed. "You had to preserve the security of the group and keep me alive. Those were your top priorities."

He nodded.

"So, what if you hadn't been in time? What if Tom had managed to kill my father?"

"It was pretty clear, after I thought about it, that if Tom killed your father you'd lose it," Marco said coolly. "Like a chess game: Tom takes your father, you take Tom. You'd have gone after Tom, exposing yourself and us. Game over. So we couldn't let that happen. Your dad had to survive for you to survive. The one expendable piece was Tom. But if anything was going to happen to Tom it would have to look natural, not like an Animorph had been involved, and not like you had been involved. It would have to be done very carefully. So, if it came down to that —"

"No," I said softly. I shook my head. I didn't want to know.

For a while neither of us said anything. I just let it sink in.

You know what Marco and I used to talk about? Whether Batman could beat Spiderman. Whether Sega was better than Nintendo. Whether some girl would rather go out with him or me.

And now . . .

"What are we, anymore, Marco? What has happened to us?"

He didn't answer. I didn't expect him to. We both knew what had happened.

"I better get back inside," I said.

"Yeah. And we need to head home. We hitched a ride on a cattle car getting here. We're hoping for something less fragrant for the return trip."

I went back toward the cabin.

CHAPTER 27

My mom was back the next day. It was Sunday, the day for Grandpa G's wake and then we had his funeral on Monday.

The local VFW chapter came and brought a bugler, who played a slow, mournful taps.

The other old soldiers took the folded American flag off the casket and gave it to my grandmother, Grandpa G's daughter.

She and the worn, grizzled men looked at each other for a long, quiet moment as if sharing a memory, a lifetime of experiences only they could understand.

I understood it, though.

Maybe not their war, but ours. Because now we're the ones out on the battle lines. The ones who fight and bleed, succeed and fail, win and lose.

We're the ones with the nightmares and the old souls.

I know what Grandpa G meant now.

He only talked about the war twice, at least to me. Once, when he opened his footlocker. And the other, that day, long ago, when we'd sat on the dock.

When my war ends, if I survive, I probably won't talk about it much, either.

As far as experiences go, once will be enough.

We each laid a rose on the casket as we left.

It wasn't a big funeral, but everyone there cried. Anyway, I did.

When we got back to the cabin we called the hospital and talked to Tom. He was doing fine.

Everything was back the way it had been. My brother still lived. So did the enemy inside him. It had all been a pointless battle. No one had wanted it, no one had profited. Everyone had suffered: Chapman, Ax, Tom, Marco, and some guy who just wanted his parking space back. And me.

But we'd all survived, and in war any time you wake up to see the sunrise it's a victory.

My folks and I drove home together on Tuesday.

I sat in the front seat with my dad while my mom dozed in the back.

Dad let me choose the radio station and told me for only about the ten millionth time how much better the music was "in his day." We had burgers for lunch and my mom told us both for only about the ten millionth time that we ate too much saturated fat. We pulled off to witness the "World's Largest Ball of Twine!" You know, except for all the other "World's Largest" twine balls.

Small, simple things, but good ones.

We talked about Grandpa G and then about other stuff.

Normal stuff.

The ride always seems shorter on the way home.

Tom had dropped the Nazi dagger in the water when he'd been knocked off the pier. I guess it had sank to the bottom of the lake.

I could have retrieved it, probably. I didn't.

But I had Grandpa G's medals in my pocket. My grandmother had given them to me. She said Grandpa G wanted me to have them.

I always knew he'd been a hero in the war. That he had medals and all. And I'd wondered why he didn't put them up in a display case, show them off for all the world to see.

But I was a little wiser, now.

Medals aren't so simple for the people who earn them. Every time Grandpa G had looked at those medals he'd thought about the things that had happened, the things he'd seen others do, the things he'd done himself.

I know he was proud of being brave, proud of doing his best for his country. But I also know why the medals were in a pouch, in a footlocker, in an attic, kept far out of sight.

Someday maybe there'll be medals for those who fought the war against the Yeerks.

I'll need to buy a footlocker.

I stood up. Looked around. Not ten feet away was this guy named Bailey. I don't know if that's his first name or last name.

"What do you want?" I demanded.

"Nothing." He shrugged.

I glared.

He blushed.

"Looking good, Rachel."

"What?"

"That leotard and all. You're looking good."

I was wearing my morphing outfit. It seemed okay for a trip around the rocks.

"Of course I look good," I snapped. "I almost always do. You have something else to say?"

I guess that threw him. He shrugged.

"Looking good," he repeated. "Looking *real* good."

"I think we've been over that," I said. "Yes, I

am good-looking. Yes, I have great hair. Yes, I have a great body. Now go away."

"You are so stuck-up!"

"That's right, I am. Now you know the difference between good looks and a good personality."

He left. I waited till he was back to a group of his friends. I scanned the other direction along the shoreline. A family with two kids, two little boys. They were coming my way but I'd have time to morph before they got close.

I began to morph.

First I shrank. Smaller and smaller. Puddles and pools rushed up toward me. A shower of spray hit me and all of a sudden it wasn't refreshing, it was scary. The force of the water nearly knocked me off my feet.

Which was easier to do since my feet were disappearing. My thighs grew thick. My arms thickened as well, forming chubby cones.

Arm, arm, leg, leg. And here was the gross part: My head was morphing to become the fifth leg. It turns out starfish don't exactly have heads. They have a mouth more or less in the middle, a bunch of wiggly little feet that look like suckers, and the five big cone legs.

That's about it for a starfish. A cockroach, by comparison, is a model of sophisticated design.

I went blind. Totally. No eyes at all.

It occurred to me to wonder how exactly I expected to find an earring when I couldn't see, but I assumed the starfish would have other compensating senses.

Nope. Not really.

It could feel. It could sort of smell. It could scoot around on its many tiny little feet. If it happened, mostly by accident, to crawl onto something tasty I guess it could eat it. But that was pretty much it for the starfish.

Well, I told myself, I *might be able to feel the earring.*

I motored my many little feet. Down, down, slithering down wet rock.

<Okay, this is stupid. An unfamiliar morph in a hole in the rock. Not your brightest move, Rachel.>

Then my foot — one of them, anyway — touched something thin and hard and round.

Amazing! I had stumbled onto the earring. It took me another ten minutes to get my useless little mouth to grab the earring. I headed back up. At least I hoped it was up.

I climbed up over the lip of the pool, out into relative dryness. I focused my mind on morphing and began to —

WHAM!

Something hit me. Hit me hard.

The starfish didn't have much in the way of

pain sensors but I still knew, the starfish knew, deep down, that it was very, very badly hurt.

I tried to make sense of it all. But all I knew for sure was this: I had been able to count to five on my starfish legs.

Now I could only count to two.

I was cut in half!

<Know the Secret>

ANIMORPHS®

K. A. Applegate

SCHOLASTIC PRESENTS

ANIMORPHS™

THE VIDEO INVASION CONTINUES PART 2

<NOWHERE TO RUN>

SPECIAL COLLECTOR'S EDITION FEATURING EXCLUSIVE, NEVER-BEFORE-SEEN FOOTAGE!

SCHOLASTIC PRESENTS

ANIMORPHS
THE INVASION SERIES

Contains Exclusive, Never-Before-Seen Footage

PART 2
< NOWHERE TO RUN >

COLLECT THEM ALL

Soccer Game Wednesday.
Math Test Friday.
Trip to the Yeerk Pool Saturday.
ANIMORPHS
Life can be hectic.
Now you can get organized.
Animorphs®
Student Planner
1999-2000
$9.95
Coming this June to
bookstores everywhere.
WARNING: Don't let it fall into the wrong hands.
Animorphs is a registered trademark of Scholastic Inc. Copyright © 1998 by K.A. Applegate. All rights reserved. Printed in the U.S.A.
ANIP11

ANIMORPHS

K. A. Applegate speaks
...and answers some FAQs.

ANIFAN: Will Tom ever get the Yeerk out of his head?

K.A.A.: Tom gets the Yeerk out of his head every three days at the Yeerk pool. Unfortunately, the Yeerk comes right back.

ANIFAN: Are any of the experiences in the books based on true happenings?

K.A.A.: I just can't think of a particular scene or character I've lifted from real life. I mean, aside from my own encounter with aliens, where they took me up into their spaceship, performed bizarre medical experiments on me, and then billed my health insurance company. (Kidding.) Wow. I guess my real life is awfully boring.

ANIFAN: When the Animorphs eat something (like Taco Bell) and then morph something small (an ant), what happens to the food?

K.A.A.: The food is extruded into Zero-space where it then becomes part of the tamale pie at your school cafeteria.

ANIFAN: Who in the world was that crazy woman Rachel met in Meg-amorphs #1?

K.A.A.: The crazy woman in the woods was actually me as I am before my morning coffee.

ANIFAN: What is ALTERNAMORPHS?

K.A.A.: This is an Animorphs branching book. You know, an interactive deal. If you guys like it there may be more books down the road.

ANIFAN: I think one of the Animorphs should morph a pig!
K.A.A.: A pig? Well, Marco's already a ham.

ANIFAN: How does Visser Three swim in the Yeerk pool? When the Yeerk is in the pool, won't Alloran slice and dice everyone?
K.A.A.: He swims in Yeerk form. When he drains out of his host body's ear, Hork-Bajir guards keep Alloran under heavy guard and restraint.

ANIFAN: Why did David turn against the Animorphs?
K.A.A.: Because he was a weak, rotten human being. You get those sometimes.

ANIFAN: Could there be more Andalites on Earth that could help the Animorphs?
K.A.A.: Actually, that's an interesting idea. Maybe someone besides Ax survived the destruction of the Dome Ship. Hmmm.

ANIFAN: Will you have any more books with the Ellimist? I think that guy is awesome.
K.A.A.: I am always worried about overusing the Ellimist. He appears in #26 and will show up again, but I need to keep him under control.

ANIFAN: How in the world did you come up with Z-space?
K.A.A.: I knew that it was impossible to exceed the speed of light anywhere in the universe, so I figured I needed a dimension that wasn't exactly part of the universe. I needed space that wasn't space: Zero-space. And thus I was awarded the Nobel Prize for Physics.

ANIFAN: Will Jake and Cassie ever go on a date???
K.A.A.: They will, in fact, get married and give birth to wolves. What? No, that can't be right.

ANIFAN: How do you manage to write one book a month, and still have time for the ANDALITE and HORK-BAJIR CHRONICLES, and still do MEGAMORPHS?
K.A.A.: A little something called coffee. Lots and lots of rich, black, French Roast coffee.

Visit the Animorphs Web site at: www.scholastic.com/animorphs

ANIMORPHS

Use the clues to unscramble the words. Then match the letters to the numbers below to read a special message from Jake.

OITHNLT

N	O	T	H	L	I	T
	2		6			

The name used to describe To-bias's state since he got stuck as a hawk.

ATPLIEESM

P	E	N	A	L	I	T	E	S
					3			11

The race that built the Chee.

RTAHET

T	H	R	E	A	T
1			8		

What the Yeerks are to human society.

DAEARL

	L			E	
	19			13	

Daughter of Prince Seerow.

GOEFRALN

E	L	F	A	N	G	O	R
				5		7	

Aximili's brother.

ORIKTSC

I	S	X	O	O	R	T
10	15		16			

One of these aliens might want to buy your memo...

ARKCYA

C	R	A	Y	A	K
	14		18		

Enemy of the Ellimist.

MAPANCH

C	H	A	P	M	A	N
			12		17	

A well-known human-Controller.

DSUT

S	T	U	D
4		9	

Marco thinks he is one.

JAKE WANTS YOU TO KNOW THAT:

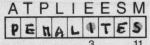

T H I S   F I G H T   I S
1 2 3 4   5 6 7 8 9 10 11

P E R S O N A L
12 13 14 15 16 17 18 19

Visit the Animorphs Web site at: www.scholastic.com/animorphs

The Reunion

Even the book morphs!
Flip the pages
and check it out!

Look for other **ANIMORPHS**®
titles by K.A. Applegate:

The Reunion

K.A. Applegate

AN
APPLE
PAPERBACK

SCHOLASTIC INC.
New York Toronto London Auckland Sydney
Mexico City New Delhi Hong Kong

No part of this publication may be reproduced in whole or in part, or stored in a retrieval system, or transmitted in any form or by any means, electronic, mechanical, photocopying, recording, or otherwise, without written permission of the publisher. For information regarding permission, write to Scholastic Inc., Attention: Permissions Department, 555 Broadway, New York, NY 10012.

ISBN 0-590-76263-X

12 11 10 9 8 7 6 5 4 3 2 1   9/9 0 1 2 3 4/0

Printed in the U.S.A.   40

First Scholastic printing, June 1999

The author wishes to thank Elise Donner
for her help in preparing this manuscript.

For Michael and Jake

The Reunion

CHAPTER 1

It was happening again. Unbelievably, it was happening again.

A woman was drowning. Not the dreaded leader of an alien force. Just a woman. Alone in a roiling sea. Defenseless. Vulnerable.

My mother.

There was no way I could let it happen again.

I powered toward her. My arms strained with each stroke. My legs kicked wildly.

Hold on. Hold on!

So close. Close enough to see her straining to keep her head above the cold black water.

Then I was on her, one arm around her shoulders, the other paddling madly to keep us afloat.

"Hold on!" I cried. "I've got you!"

She looked up at me, wet hair plastering her face. Then she spoke. "Thank you, Marco."

"Mom . . ."

"I'm free, Marco. I'm free!"

And then a powerful current swept her out of my grasp and sucked her under the glittering surface of the midnight ocean.

"No! No, no, no!"

I dove. The salt stung my eyes. I pushed deeper and deeper into the darkness. My lungs ached but I would not allow it to happen again. I would not let her go! Not when she was free. Not . . .

"NO!"

"Marco? Are you okay?"

I shot up straight as a board. Where . . . ? My bed, my room. My father.

I put my hands to my head and looked at the picture of my mother that sat on my nightstand.

"You okay?" he repeated.

No. I wasn't. "Yeah. Yeah. Bad dream, I guess."

"About her?"

I swallowed hard. "Yeah."

Dad sat on the edge of my bed and hugged me.

I returned the hug weakly. Patted him on the back.

"I'm okay, big guy," I said. "What time is it?"

"About time to get up and get going," he said. "I get the shower first. I have to be in early today."

I watched my father leave the room. But instead of getting out of bed and heading downstairs for a bowl of Honeycomb, I sat amidst the tangled, slightly damp bedcovers, too exhausted to move.

My name, as you probably know by now, is Marco. And that was how my Friday started. Not the greatest way to greet the last day of a long week. But not exactly uncommon. Dreams of fear and loss and despair.

Before I lost my mother to the enemy, before I learned of the Yeerk invasion of Earth, my life was pretty tame. Mostly I worried about things like whether I'd dropped enough hints at dinner about which Sega disk I wanted for my birthday.

Not about things like the enslavement of the human race.

Those were the days. Or, as Dad says, "The salad days."

I'm not sure what that means exactly — "salad days" — but he says it a lot. I'm not a big fan of salad myself, unless it's heavily croutoned.

Anyway, here's the rough sequence of events. I'll keep it brief.

My mother — my beautiful, pretty-smelling, intelligent mother — took our boat out late one night and never came back. They found the boat. They didn't find her.

She was presumed drowned. With no explanation of why she had done such a strange thing like take the boat out alone. At night. I mean, my mother was not exactly the suicidal type.

Next. My friends — Jake, Rachel, Cassie, and Tobias — and I had the distinct misfortune to stumble upon a dying Andalite warrior prince who told us about the Yeerks and their invasion of our planet. He gave us the gift and curse of morphing, an Andalite technology that allows us to acquire the DNA of any animal and become — morph — that animal.

This is our most spectacular weapon. The others are cunning, courage, and secrecy. (And in my case irresistible cuteness.)

Then, we were joined by Aximili-Esgarrouth-Isthill, younger brother of Prince Elfangor.

Another highlight. This happened long after I'd learned my mother had not fallen overboard and drowned but had been infested by the Yeerk known as Visser One, originator of the Earth invasion. I'm talking about the time I'd seen her frail, Yeerk-infested body floating facedown as the Yeerks' underwater headquarters destructed.

Since that moment I've spent at least, oh, a

bazillion hours wondering if my mother could have survived. Rachel heard a submarine speeding away from the chaotic scene. And I'd seen a Leeran-Controller swimming toward my mother's floating body. So there was a chance she'd lived, a chance the Leeran had dragged her unconscious body to the sub and powered away.

At least, that's what I chose to believe. But alongside that belief was the realization that the chances she'd made it to the sub were slim.

You can understand how sometimes my particular daily grind gets to be a pain in the . . .

I mean, five more or less normal kids, one of whom is now more bird than boy, plus an Andalite cadet are supposed to save the Earth from an army of evil sluglike parasites?

What are the odds that's going to happen?

The Yeerks are parasitic. They squirm their way into your ear canal and from there seep into every nook and cranny of your brain. They assume total control over your thoughts and your actions. They leave you alert and alive — but absolutely powerless to act or speak on your own behalf. You are locked in a kind of brain cage while the Yeerk takes over every single aspect of your life. The Yeerk is in total control.

Total control.

The Yeerk moves your eyes and hands and

5

feet. The Yeerk speaks with your voice. The Yeerk opens your memories and reads them like a book. Every memory. Every secret.

The Yeerk in my mother's head can look through her memories and see what she saw as she comforted me in my crib long, long ago. The Yeerk can see memories of me crying from a skinned knee. Memories of grouchy breakfasts with my dad and me. Memories of the hideously embarrassing "birds and bees" conversation.

The Yeerk saw all of that. The Yeerk who held the rank of Visser One. The original overlord of the invasion of Earth. The Yeerk who made a slave of my mother.

Because of this invasion our lives have become a series of fierce battles and narrow escapes. Of soul-crushing experiences and bone-shattering fights. You can see why my mornings have taken a dramatic turn for the worse.

Just the same, when Dad left for work, I took a shower and got ready with every intention of going to school.

Really, I did.

CHAPTER 2

With a clean face and conditioned hair I headed toward the school bus stop.

And walked past it.

Instead, I hopped on a city bus headed downtown.

The warren of streets that is the financial and business center of our town seemed as good a place as any to kill time. To get lost without running the risk of running into anyone who knew me.

There were movie theaters downtown. I figured I'd look around till I could catch a matinee of something loud and fun.

Twenty minutes later the bus dropped me and

thirty office-bound men and women in the heart of blue-suit central.

It was still way early but already the sun was heating up the sidewalks, and the exhaust from the cars, trucks, and buses was spread like a grubby, smelly blanket over the concrete and steel jungle.

Nice choice, Marco. I should have gone to the beach. I stood on the sidewalk and stared.

Seething mass of humanity. I'd heard that phrase once and now I knew what it meant. It meant "office workers at rush hour."

What was the big hurry? Did adults really like going to work? Or was Friday free donut day at the office?

THWACK!

I was down! My knees hit the pavement and my face landed in a planter full of cigarette butts and abandoned coffee cups.

The enemy! I prepared myself for the next blow.

Nothing. I looked up.

No one had noticed I'd been knocked over.

I got to my feet, dazed. I rubbed the ash, dirt, and stale coffee off my face with the bottom of my shirt.

I was disgusted. And I was mad.

A woman had run me over with her tank of a briefcase. Then she'd continued on down the street like nothing had happened. And no one had stopped to help me.

"And they say *my* generation has no manners," I muttered.

I gave myself a quick once-over — nothing seriously damaged but my dignity — and set out after the woman who'd so callously whacked me. This woman had an appointment with the dirty pavement, courtesy of a well-placed Saucony Cross Trainer.

I caught up to her about halfway down the block and followed a few feet behind. Waiting for my chance. Her briefcase was big enough to hold a Doberman and built to maim, with steel corners and a big combination lock on the side.

And what was up with that hair? The woman wore a stiff, curly blonde wig. Think steel-wool pad. Used. Slightly shredded. And yellow.

I saw the perfect spot to exact my revenge.

I skirted the crowd and hid behind a big, concrete column about a yard ahead, just at the corner of the courthouse. When Wig Lady passed — bingo, bango! BAM!

She was going down.

I peeked from around the pillar to see how close she was to meeting my foot. And then I bit my cheek to stop from screaming.

The woman with the awful blonde hair and the briefcase . . .

Was my mother!

Visser One!

I ducked back behind the column and pulled my South Park cap down over my eyes. She passed by. She hadn't seen me.

My mother was alive!

I took a deep breath and tried to comprehend this fact. She'd escaped the destruction of the Yeerk underwater complex. Relief and happiness and fear all at once. She was alive! But she was so dangerous. So terribly dangerous.

Think, Marco. She's alive, but . . . the disguise. A blue power suit. A curly blonde wig. What had looked like blue contact lenses behind big, black-rimmed glasses. The massive briefcase.

Why a disguise? To hide. From whom?

Should I follow her? Find the others? I could still make it to school before the late bell. Maybe.

But then I'd lose my mother for sure. And Visser One.

I watched my mother's body walk down the street. When she reached the next corner, I followed.

On the next block I saw her climb the steps to the front doors of the Sutherland Tower, the downtown area's tallest building. She squeezed herself and her briefcase into a compartment of the revolving door. I bolted up the steps, waited one extra revolution of the brass-plated door, then followed her in.

The lobby was about three stories tall. Behind a row of security guards, water flowed down one pink marble wall into a lit pool. Visser One flashed some kind of pass and continued by the guard's station.

I had no pass. Plus I was a kid. The guards had already seen me come in, and now they were looking at me like I was one hundred percent no-good. If I made the wrong move they were sure to hassle me. Then the Visser would look over her shoulder to see what the commotion was about and I'd be in big, big trouble.

Visser One would recognize me as her host body's son.

So I stood. Just stopped right there by the re-volving door and waited for the next person to come through.

Whoever it was, their DNA was mine.

CHAPTER 3

The revolving door whooshed. Footsteps behind me. I turned around.

"Hi, Dad!" I said. "What took you so long?"

The man was stocky, well-dressed, and surprised. But he had his ID in one hand and I had his other hand and before he knew it, the mild acquisition trance was in place.

"Hello, Mr. Grant," said a slick-haired security guard.

"It's 'Fathers Take Their Sons to Work Day!'" I said brightly as I led the zoned-out Mr. Grant past security.

"Well, then, son, you pay attention! That's one important daddy you got!"

"Yessir!" I replied.

The boyish enthusiasm worked like a charm. I've found that if you act like a moron, adults tend to leave you alone. It's when they think you might be as smart as they are that they give you a hard time.

I led Mr. Grant to the elevator. Let me make it clear that I had no intention of morphing this man. I just needed him to get me past security and to the elevators.

Where Visser One was standing with her enormous metal case.

Mr. Grant was waking up. I let go of his hand.

"My," he muttered, putting his hand on his stomach. "That jelly donut is not sitting well."

I looked up at Mr. Grant with an Adam Sandler idiot grin.

Worked like a charm. Mr. Grant looked away and waited impatiently for the elevator with the rest of the men and woman in suits.

I pulled my hat lower over my face.

DING! The elevator door opened. An old guy with a rolling cart full of interoffice envelopes and UPS packages made an attempt to get out of the car.

"Let 'em off, people!" he muttered as the crowd surged around him and into the elevator.

Visser One passed on the mail guy's right. I went to his left. The mob prevented her from getting a glimpse of me.

13

The doors closed. We were packed in the elevator like crayons in a crayon box. The important thing was Visser One was the crayon close to the button panel, and I was the crayon in the opposite back corner.

But that's not good, I thought suddenly. I have to get out when my mom . . . the Visser gets out! If I miss the floor, I lose the Visser. And my mother. Again.

At the same time, I couldn't allow Visser One to see me. There was only one thing I could do. A morph. In the slow-moving elevator. Surrounded by fifteen people and evil incarnate.

A woman whose back was about three inches from the bill of my baseball cap dropped a section of her *Wall Street Journal* and I pretended not to notice. I slid down against the elevator wall, back straight, and with my fingertips, picked it up off the grubby red carpet. Behind the suited backs of fifteen adults, I opened the paper as wide as I could and held it in front of my face and over my head, like a tent. And then I began one of my least favorite morphs — the common housefly.

Insane! It was insane. But what was my other choice? Lose Visser One? No. Not happening.

I started shrinking almost immediately. In a moment, the newspaper blanketed me. My vision went dark and then flashed on again, pixilated.

Two fly legs spurted from my chest. My hands shriveled into pincers. My skin hardened.

And nobody noticed. It was bizarre! No one looked at me. Everyone continued to stare blankly ahead at the door or up at the ventilation grates on the roof of the elevator car.

I was in an elevator full of people, turning into a fly, and no one so much as glanced back at me. I fought down the lunatic urge to say, "Hey, I'm turning into a fly, here. Hello? Are you people or statues?"

The elevator slowed and stopped at a floor. The woman who had dropped the paper earlier bent to pick it up.

Problem. I wasn't done morphing!

I was about the size of a rat, with pink skin and a human nose. The other nine-tenths of me was housefly. Wings, six hairy legs, compound eyes, a big sticky tongue where my mouth had been. And I was sitting in the middle of a mound of clothes.

A more disgusting sight I cannot imagine.

The woman picked up the paper, stared back at a piece of nothing two feet above the head of the person in front of her, then froze.

"Argh!" she said.

Through my 360-degree multifaceted fly vision I watched her look slowly back down to the dirty red carpet. But it was too late.

15

Totally fly now, I kicked on my wings, zoomed crazily into the air, sped over the woman's head and landed on a corner of the Visser's briefcase. The elevator door opened. The woman who was positive she had just seen a rat-sized fly-boy on the elevator floor rushed out with her hand to her mouth.

A few other business people filed out after her and the Visser pressed the CLOSE button.

The twenty-first floor. Mr. Grant got off.

The Visser pushed CLOSE once more.

And I was alone in the elevator with my mother.

Twenty-second floor. The elevator slid to a stop. The doors opened and Visser One stepped out into the hallway. I rode on her briefcase to where she stopped just outside the third door on the right.

It was all I needed to know. Time to get out of there and tell the others.

CHAPTER 4

I let go with my sticky, pincher fly feet. I buzzed my gossamer wings and lifted up off the Visser's metal case.

Up, circle back and away toward . . .

SCHLOOOOP!

Wind! A tornado of wind!

My wings beat with a speed only an insect could achieve. But I was too close! A vent, ribbed steel, as high as a ten-story building to me, and twice as wide.

Air cleaner! Industrial-strength. Suction. Suction like a vacuum cleaner!

WHAM!

I hit a metal crossbar.

Then I was through. Hurtling down an alu-

17

minum shaft. And now, concentrated in the enclosed space, the air current was unbelievable.

<Aaaagh!>

I was spinning, out of control, wings almost useless. And I wasn't alone. Pieces of lint and human hair. Dust and the circles of paper a three-hole puncher leaves behind. An assortment of dazed mosquitoes, gnats, and other flies, all zooming around me like the tornado scene from *The Wizard of Oz.* All of it shattered into the thousand tiny TV sets of my fly eyes. All of it in weird, distorted colors.

I tumbled faster and faster toward a giant filter. Bundles of flying-bug parts and lint were scattered at its base. There was only one thing to do.

Demorph!

I started growing almost immediately and almost immediately I stopped tumbling. Anything over the weight of a flicked booger pretty much canceled out the power of the industrial-strength air cleaner.

My wings shriveled and sucked into the now-supple skin under my shoulder blades. My eyes rotated from the sides of my head back to the front of my face. Two fly legs shot back into my chest.

FLOOP! FLOOP!

My other fly legs rotated to where my human

legs and arms should be and everything started to grow. Suddenly, I realized that the aluminum shaft that had seemed as big as the school gym when I was a fly just might not be big enough for my human self.

Getting trapped like a big chunk of Snicker's Blizzard in a straw was something I was not prepared for.

I pushed my now-human arms in front of me and thrust my legs behind me. I lay fully extended on my stomach in the air shaft.

And then I stopped demorphing. I was me. For once, I was grateful to be a little on the short side.

Still, I was trapped inside a very dusty air vent.

I slithered down the square metal tube, away from the filter, toward a light beaming across the shaft. I pushed myself forward with my toes and pulled myself along with my fingers, trying hard not to panic.

The light was coming from a vent high on the wall of an office. I gave the grate a whack and it opened downward like a miniature door. I was a good eight or nine feet in the air. I lowered myself headfirst, slowly, slowly . . .

Keys jingled outside the door.

I dropped fast, forcing myself into a head-over-heels tumble as I fell.

BAM!

Right into a wastebasket.

"Three points," I whispered to myself.

The door to the office opened just as I scurried into the second room, a big, windowless space full of gray cubicles.

"Hello?" Lights popped on. "Mr. Grant?"

Footsteps. Slow, but coming my way.

I had no choice! I had to morph Mr. Grant.

I dashed into an empty cubicle at the back of the room and felt the changes begin.

Morphing a fly may be gross, but morphing a human being is far more frightening. Not to mention morally suspect. In this case, morphing an adult male was like getting an unwanted glimpse into my own future and realizing that my future was not pretty.

The first thing to change was my stomach. It grew out and around until the seams of my morphing suit began to tear.

My thick, gorgeous hair was sucked into my broadening skull. I slapped a hand to my head. A receding hairline! A balding spot right on top!

I watched as the skin on my hands wrinkled slightly. Pale blotches sprinkled themselves across the knuckles. I touched my face with the ugly fingers. Wow! Rough . . . At this rate I'd have a five o'clock shadow by noon!

Riiiiip!

My butt! I turned my double-chinned neck as far as it would turn and saw over my thick shoulder a wide protuberance — and my bike shorts in shreds.

Panic set in. I was pretty sure I hadn't grown taller but man, had I gotten wider!

"Mr. Grant?"

"Yes?" I yelped, sticking my balding, slightly grizzled head over the cubicle partition.

The woman stood in the doorway of the second room.

"Uh, are you okay, Mr. Grant?" She took another step inside.

"No!" I shouted. "I mean, don't come in. I'm very busy. I'm just fine."

"You were working in the dark Mr. Grant. Are you sure . . ."

"Yes, I'm just fine, thanks. I'll be done here in a few minutes," I babbled.

Another step closer. "Why are you at Carlos's desk?"

Good one. I thought fast. "Uh, well, there's something wrong with my computer, so, uh, I thought I'd borrow this one. Uh, could you get me a cup of coffee from the Starbucks on the corner? Please?"

The woman's eyebrows quirked but she turned and headed for the door. "Sure, Mr. Grant. I'll be right back."

"Thanks, thanks a lot!" I said, ducking back behind the cubicle partition.

Yow! Too close. I waited until I hoped the woman had gotten on the elevator and sprinted from the cubicle. Time to find a place safe to demorph and get the heck out of this building.

The men's room. I flung open the door to the hallway. And ran smack into . . .

"Aaahh!" I yelled. "Mr. Grant!"

"What the . . ." was all he got out before he slumped to the floor.

I shot a glance up and down the hallway. No one.

"Oh man, oh man, Jake is gonna kill me, and if *he* doesn't, Cassie will." I hefted Mr. Grant to a half-sitting position and dragged him across the hall and into a broom closet. It was like moving one of those stones they used to build the pyramids. The man liked his pastry.

I shut the door behind us and tried to catch my breath. Hard to do when you're panicking on several fronts simultaneously.

I propped him up against a mop bucket on wheels and started to undress him.

Quickly, I changed into Mr. Grant's blue suit. Well, all except the tie. I have no idea how to tie one.

When I was dressed I opened the broom closet

door, looked both ways, then scooted as fast as Mr. Grant could to the elevator.

A moment later the elevator doors slid open and I burst inside.

I was outta there.

CHAPTER 5

It was almost lunch period by the time I'd gone home, changed, and got back to school.

Now, getting into school late is not the easiest thing in the world to do, but it can be done. Luckily, our school has no guards or metal detectors like they have in the high schools. All I had to worry about was the stray teacher or kiss-up hall monitor.

I leaned around the front door. Nobody. Just the janitor, but his back was to me and he was wearing headphones. And doing this weird kind of shuffling dance as he pushed a mop across the vomit-green linoleum tile that is our school's main hallway.

I slid around the doorjamb and booked the

other way down the main hall. I could see the tops of teachers' heads through the windows in the classroom doors, but knew they couldn't see me. Another benefit of being vertically challenged.

I made it to my locker undetected. A second later, the bell for lunch period rang and the halls were mobbed by kids charging out of class. One of them was Jake. I dropped my math book. He picked it up.

"Jake, you really do care."

"Where have you been?" he demanded.

"Guess who I saw?" I whispered, pulling a notebook at random from my locker.

Jake sighed. "Marco, just tell me . . ."

"Marco!"

A hand clapped onto my shoulder.

"So nice of you to join us today."

"My pleasure, Mr. Chapman," I said. "I would never want to miss a day of learning."

Jake gave me a "This-is-*your*-problem" look and sauntered away.

"Ah, amusing as always, Marco. And where might you have been? I called your home. No answer. No answer at all."

"I was . . . with my father."

"Oh, really?"

"Yes, Mr. Chapman. It was 'Take Your Son to Work Day' at his office."

"Then I suppose you won't mind me calling him at work?"

"Not at all," I bluffed. "Would you like the number?"

Chapman looked me up and down. If he called my dad, I was busted, big time.

"He'll be in meetings all afternoon, that's why I came back to school," I added. "But you could leave a message on his voice mail."

"Just get where you're supposed to be, Marco."

"Yes, sir."

I should have said "Yes, you Yeerk-carrying freak." But that would have been fatal. To me.

Telling Jake about Visser One would have to wait. In the cafeteria I passed a note to Rachel.

Barn. After school. Good news and bad.

I sat at the end of a lunch table and ate my pizza alone.

Ignored the minor food fight going on at the table to my right. Vaguely noticed the pimply kid slurping some gross yellow soup from a plaid thermos at the other end of my table. Thought for two seconds about the history test I was going to fail that afternoon. Wondered if Chapman was going to bring up my cutting school and failing my history test at the next parent-teacher conference. Considered whether I'd rather spend my life working at McDonald's or Burger King after I got expelled.

But my mind wouldn't stay on any one topic. Nothing really mattered, did it? Nothing except one extraordinarily complicated, amazingly wonderful fact.

My mother was alive.

Alive.

I saw Rachel giving me the fish eye from across the room. I mouthed that one word: *alive.*

Evidently Rachel doesn't read lips. She misunderstood what I'd said and responded by mouthing two words I won't repeat.

But I didn't care. No one could blow this one moment of relief for me.

She was alive. And someday, somehow, by some miracle I could only fantasize about, she'd be my mom again.

CHAPTER 6

"Marco," Cassie said, "tell us why we're here."

"We" being four kids, a bird, and a furry blue alien. Freaks is our name, saving the world is our game.

"This morning I skipped school and took the bus downtown." I shot a look at Jake. "And before anyone jumps down my throat, I know it's dumb to call attention to myself, so sue me. Anyway, I was trying to avoid being trampled by the wing tips when I saw my . . . Visser One. She was in disguise. A terrible wig, blue contacts, and big square glasses. But it was her."

"Oh, man," Jake said. "Are you sure it was your mother?"

"Oh, yeah. I got a great look at her right before I was going to trip her."

"You were going to trip your mother?" said Cassie.

"Yes, because she'd knocked me down with this big metal briefcase. It doesn't matter. What matters is that it was Visser One. My mother. In disguise."

"You're sure she didn't recognize you and knock you down on purpose?" Rachel demanded.

"Yeah," I said. "Anyway, she thinks I'm a Controller. Remember when we went after the Yeerks' underwater complex? Don't forget: We spoke. She thinks I'm one of them. So why would she smack me, unprovoked? And if she knew the truth about me, she'd have done more than just knock me down."

"And what *was* the brilliant motive behind skipping school?"

"I'm an adventurer, Rachel," I said. "Much like Daniel Boone. Magellan. Marco Polo. I will not rest until I have explored every alley, every nook, every cranny of this big, crazy world of ours."

"Not funny, Mr. Polo," she snapped. "You could have gotten us in big trouble. . . ."

<What is a cranny, exactly?> Tobias wondered from his perch above us.

<So. Visser One is alive,> Ax said coldly. <This is not good news.>

29

"The corollary, Ax. My mother's alive, too," I pointed out. "I followed her into the Sutherland Tower. She's got an office on the twenty-second floor."

"What do you think she's doing in there?" Cassie said.

I shook my head. "I didn't stick around to find out."

"The last time we saw Visser One," Jake mused, "Visser Three saw us — the enemy — spare her life."

<If Visser Three understood that we spared Visser One, he would conclude that she is a traitor,> Ax said.

"Which explains the disguise," I agreed. "But she'd still need access to a Yeerk pool. To Kandrona rays. Which Visser Three wouldn't allow if he thought she was a traitor. Obviously. So . . ."

"So somehow she's alive, somehow she's getting Kandrona rays," Rachel said.

"The question is why?" Cassie said.

"Why what?"

"Why is she here, on Earth? Look, we know going way back that Vissers One and Three are enemies. Visser One let us escape from Visser Three early on. Visser Three must have suspected she was behind that. Then he's got the fact that we let her live when we could have finished her off. So he must want her bad. So why is she walking around downtown? I mean, wig or no wig, Earth isn't a safe place for her."

Rachel grinned. "Come on, it's obvious. She's here to take down Visser Three. Why else? It's her only way out. Take down her main enemy. Then get herself straight with whoever is above them both."

I nodded. It made sense. Figure Rachel to understand the mind of Visser One.

"Whatever her exact motives, it's bad news for us," Cassie said.

"Not necessarily," Jake said. "Warring Vissers are a lot easier to handle than Vissers united against us."

<Divide and conquer,> Ax agreed. <We may be able to use the feud between the Vissers to our advantage.>

Jake nodded. "First step, find out what's in that office."

"She's on twenty-two, third door to the right off the elevator," I said.

<We might be able to gain access from the roof,> Ax suggested.

"Tobias?"

<Yeah, I know the Sutherland Tower,> he said. <There's a door on the roof that probably opens on a staircase leading to the top-floor hall. There's a padlock but the door's pretty rickety. We should have no problem getting in.>

31

"Fly morph?" Cassie said. "Up to the roof as a bird, demorph, morph a fly . . ."

"Not recommended. I had a bad experience with the ventilation system today. But a fast, heavier bug would work, one that can go under doors and through walls."

"You mean . . ."

"That's right." I grinned. "Everyone's favorite houseguest. The wily cockroach."

"We do this right away," Jake directed. "Tonight. But I'm out. Family function."

"Me, too," Rachel said, rolling her eyes. "I promised my mother I'd baby-sit for Jordan and Sara. And I have blown my mom off way too much lately."

"I hate to do this," Cassie said, "but I'm out, too. I am one test away from a 'D' in math. If I get a 'D' my parents will be in my life twenty-four hours a day."

<Ax and I are available,> Tobias said. <No families, no homes, nothing to do but watch the owls eat my mice. Ax-man and I will handle this.>

"And me, obviously," I said.

Jake looked at me.

"What about your dad?" Cassie asked quickly. She was trying to give me an out.

"What about him? He's been working twelve-hour days on a big project. He comes home, he plops on the couch, he watches ESPN. He'll never know I'm gone."

Jake continued to look at me. Rachel looked away.

<There's the problem of Visser One inhabiting your mother's body,> Ax stated bluntly. <And the temptations that seeing her again might arouse.>

Leave it to Ax to be blunt.

"Ax is right, Marco," Cassie said. "Coming face-to-face with Visser One again will be hard for you. And dangerous. For all of us."

"Did I give myself away on the Royan Island mission?" I demanded. "Or today?"

"First time, pretty close," Rachel muttered.

"No, not pretty close," I snapped. "I *didn't*. And that's the fact."

There was an awkward silence.

"I don't believe this crap," I said. "We've been through this before. The mission comes first. Personal hang-ups, second. I'm in. I'm going. Period."

Jake sighed. "Okay, Marco, Ax, and Tobias. Tonight." He looked at me. "Don't do anything foolish. It's reconnaissance only."

I nodded.

"And if it comes to a judgment call, Tobias makes the call."

That caught me off guard. But there was no point arguing. In Jake's place I'd have done the same thing.

"No problem."

Jake came and took my arm and drew me with him outside into the afternoon sunlight. I cringed. I knew what was coming.

"I noticed a certain lack of details about what happened today," Jake said. "Which tells me you did things that I probably don't want to hear about."

"Yeah. You probably don't." I tried out a devil-may-care grin. Not a big success.

Jake folded his arms over his chest and looked down at the ground in silence. Then up at me.

Jake has changed a lot over the months we've been fighting this little war. The look he gave me did not come from my boy Jake, my bud, my pal. It came from a battle commander.

Freaky seeing how old Jake has gotten.

"Marco, you're my best friend. But if you ever go off like that again you and I will have serious problems."

In the old days I'd have said "Bite me," or something equally brilliant.

Now I said, "Okay, understood."

It was all I could do to stop myself from saying, "Yes, sir."

CHAPTER 7

At eleven-thirty that night, with my dad safely snoring in his room, I morphed to seagull and flew to one of the little urban parks scattered throughout the downtown area. Benches, shrubs, trash cans, a few spindly trees. A place where the suits go to eat their bagel sandwiches.

I landed on the dusty ground to pick through the bounty that is an overturned garbage can when I heard the call of a bird of prey. Reluctantly I turned away from the remains of a gyro and took off to join a red-tailed hawk coming in from the north and a northern harrier, coming from the south.

A scavenger like the seagull are good flyers, low and fast. But not nearly as good as hawks and harriers. Too fat from gorging on hot dogs and clams, maybe. By the time I joined Ax and Tobias on the roof of the Sutherland Tower, I was exhausted from pushing for all that altitude.

<The light's not on in the office,> Tobias said.

<She's there,> I said confidently. She had to be. <Let's try that door.>

The door Tobias had told us about earlier wasn't keeping anyone out, least of all a roach. Clearly at one point someone had pried his way in with a crowbar, leaving gouges plenty wide for even a hefty seagull.

But roach was the way to go.

They say that after the big one, total nuclear annihilation, when every other living thing has been turned into a pile of glowing mud, roaches will still be powering over the ruins of civilization.

The amazing indestructible roach. They adapt almost immediately to whatever poison is unleashed on them. And they eat virtually anything — books, glue, plants, dead fish, old sneakers. It's almost impossible to destroy them.

I like that about cockroaches.

The wind was whipping. Heavy clouds covered the moon and the stars. Only the lights on in the surrounding buildings pierced the gloom. We were three mutants on a depressing, deserted island in the sky. An acre of tarred gravel and air-conditioning machinery surrounded us. There was a flagpole, no flag. The hoist kept slapping the pole with a sort of hollow twang.

The sight of Ax halfway between Andalite and cockroach was more interesting than disturbing. Like an armadillo from planet Kill-or-Be-Killed. A cat-sized beetle with a shell made of steel and six roach legs, each with an Andalite hoof. Add to that a foot-long tail with a spike made to stab and you have one mean-looking being.

Tobias, on the other hand, looked disgusting.

Red-tailed hawks and cockroaches were not meant to merge. You've got absolute majesty on the one hand and absolute utility on the other. Mother Nature didn't come up with a birdbug on her own for good reason.

Tobias's beak had transformed into a jaw, opening and shutting involuntarily. Pencil-size antennae jutted from his head. Two hairy stumps poked from the sides of his hawk neck. His wings had molted and shifted onto his back. I watched as they hardened into translucent shell. Below them I could see roach wings growing out of the top of his head.

I shuddered and started my own morph. Focused on all that was roach. Garbage, dark corners, bathrooms, opened cereal boxes . . .

My skin hardened first, scalp to toes.

My arms fused to my sides, then migrated to my back.

Four legs crept out of my sides and I fell forward. The floor had already been getting closer and closer as I shrank to the size of a quarter.

My vision pixilated. Compound roach eyes, with about two thousand lenses, were in place.

My antennae twitched as the roach's amazing sense of smell surged to life. Roaches can smell everything. Good smells like bacon frying. Bad smells like dog poop.

The roof smelled like tar and electricity and cigarette butts.

My innards lost definition and became one long intestinal tract. My mouth lost its lips. My tongue gravitated back into my throat and became a crop, a kind of second mouth.

And then the roach brain turned on. I was in the open.

Way open.

No shelter! No protection!

Fear! Fear! Fear!

I charged ahead and narrowly missed ramming another cockroach. I turned, scrambled across the tar paving of the roof, skittered across a pile of broken glass, and launched. I did an Evel Knievel into Ax.

<Marco, Tobias, I believe you may be in the grip of the cockroach instincts,> Ax said.

<Oh, and you're not?> Tobias countered. <I see you: You're six inches up the flagpole!>

<Okay, okay, everyone stop,> I said. <Nobody move. Where are we heading?>

<The door. Which is . . . well . . .>

Ten minutes later we found our way back to the door. We crept through the ravaged door and skittered wildly down the steps.

There are two ways a roach can go down a set of stairs. It can climb across each tread and down each riser, or it can simply leap off each step and land on the step below.

Unfortunately, we had a lot of steps to go to get down to the twenty-second floor.

So I suggested a third possibility.

CHAPTER 8

<The railing is continuous,> I pointed out. <We could race down along the railing.>

<What if we fall off?> Tobias asked.

<We land on the steps, big deal,> I said.

<What if we fall off to the right?>

I was afraid he was going to bring that up. Roach eyes couldn't see that far but I was pretty sure it was a straight drop all the way down. <Then we find out just how far a roach can fall without getting killed.>

<We do have to watch our time in morph,> Tobias said.

The railing was cylindrical painted steel. A bar welded here and there, but basically snaking downward in a long, steep series of tight ovals.

Climbing it was hard. Even for a roach. The paint was slick. Fortunately, it had been painted many times and the cracks and runs of many paint jobs gave us footholds.

Still, it was like climbing the Washington Monument. At the top we scrambled over onto the railing itself.

Picture one of those Olympic ski jumps. Only you can't see well enough to see the end. And it's curved, so you can slide off left or right. And if it's right you are going to fall for about three days.

I was in the lead.

<I think we just go for it,> I said. <I mean, all out instead of creeping along.>

<Twenty floors,> Tobias said. <Two turns equal a floor. Forty turns.>

<I will keep track,> Ax offered.

Ax has no faith in our human ability to do simple things like count. With good reason.

<The horses are at the starting gate,> I said. <And . . . they're off!>

I motored my roach legs and rocketed down the railing.

<Aaaaahhhhhh!>

Zooooooom!

Down the railing!

You think a roach looks fast from five feet up as you're trying to stomp it on the kitchen floor? It looks a lot faster down at roach level.

My face was a millimeter off the "ground." Like being strapped facedown underneath someone's Porsche.

My legs were splayed too wide, so that with each of my steps, each of my six legs slipped off into the air. The result was a sort of lurching, out-of-control run that had me skinning along on my belly half the time.

<Aaaahhhhh!> Tobias yelled from behind me.

<First turn!> I yelled.

I hit the turn going at what felt like two hundred miles an hour. I slid to my right to catch the banked corner.

It was total toboggan. It was the luge with rockets strapped to your butt. It was a ride that a skateboarder would have traded his kidneys for.

Down at insane speed, feet motoring, slipping, belly skinning, antennae whipping back. The "road" was a balance beam that had been replaced by a pipe.

It was insane!

<Turn!>

I whipped into a second turn, and now my momentum had taken over. There was no stopping. There was no slowing down. We were out of control. We were projectiles, barely making contact with the steel, banking into 5g turns that would have dropped our guts out through our toes. If we'd had guts. Or toes.

Floor after floor! Bare escape after bare escape. Skittering, scrabbling, fighting, running like someone who's being dragged behind a bus.

<Two more turns and we are there,> Ax yelled.

<What do we do?>

<Jump!>

<Jump? When?>

<NOW!> Ax yelled.

CHAPTER 9

I went into the final turn. No banking this time. It was time for the sled to go off the path while the announcer said, "Oh! Ladies and gentlemen, there's been a terrible accident; I hope everyone's okay!"

I hit the turn. I did not drop down to take the turn. I kept motoring, straight ahead. Straight ahead and suddenly my little roach feet were motoring on air.

<Aaaaahhhhh!>

I fell.

I fell a long way.

Plop!

I hit the floor.

Plop! Plop!

Ax and Tobias landed nearby.

<You okay?>

<Yeah. Ax-man?>

<I am fine.>

<That was cool!> I said.

<Way cool!> Tobias agreed.

<Let's never, *ever* do that again!> I said.

<Never. Ever.>

<Repetition of that activity would be a very bad idea,> Ax agreed.

We scooted over to, then under a fire door, with the steel scraping our backs, and into the hallway of the twenty-second floor.

The hall was dark except for a weak ray of light from the bottom of a closed door just ahead. We raced along the industrial carpet, hugging the wall.

Then the door to the lighted office opened.

A man stepped out and the hall lights went on.

Panic!

<Nobody move!>

We stood stock-still as the looming figure took another step.

"IRS and their audits," the man muttered.

He turned the lights off and locked the door behind him. Then he went ballistic.

"Roach!" he cried. I felt the violent vibration of his massive human foot slam down on the carpet.

<Ax! Tobias!>

<I am right behind you, Marco,> Ax replied.

<I think he got a *real* roach,> Tobias said. <Just stay put. Freeze!>

The man walked toward the elevator, muttering about how much rent he was paying for his office and there were roaches and they said it was a luxury building, hah!

There was a DING announcing the elevator's arrival. The hall lights went off. The elevator door closed. We were alone on the twenty-second floor.

Except, of course, for my mom.

No, not my mom, I told myself. I couldn't start thinking that way.

She was Visser One. That's who we were up against.

We scurried on until we reached what I was pretty sure was the door to the Visser's office. Up along the doorjamb, then across the surface of the door to the base of the window set in the center.

The roach's vision was not so spectacular. Still, I could make out enough of the room to decide it looked like a normal office. A reception desk, a plush chair, a leather couch, phones, computer, printer, a copy machine, a coffee-maker.

Nothing Yeerk about it at all.

<Perhaps we have the wrong location,> Ax said.

<I know I saw her go in here this morning.>

<We've got to go in. I didn't just survive the roller coaster from hell to turn around and give up.> Tobias said as he led the way. We skittered back down the door and tried to squeeze under it. No luck.

<An impenetrable seal,> Ax noted. <Probably around the entire doorframe.>

<No one puts this tight a seal around an average office door.> I sighed. <Looks like the air vent's our best bet.>

I led the way up the wall and through the air vent I'd been sucked into that morning.

<Which way?> Tobias asked.

<I'm guessing to the right.>

We scrambled through scatterings of lint and ash to a vent that opened into what had to be the Visser's lair. Assuming the Visser was preparing to go to war with a small country.

<Hologram paint,> Ax explained. <One can paint a window, project a hologram onto the back of this paint, and thereby disguise a room. The Visser has projected the picture of a normal office onto the back of the paint. Very clever.>

<So anyone who passes by, like a security guard, won't know what's going down in here,> Tobias added.

<It's got to be on the exterior windows, too,> I surmised. <To fool window washers.>

<Or red-tailed hawks. Let's do this quick and get out of here.>

In almost total darkness we crawled out through the grate and along the ceiling until we reached a wall. Then down the wall and onto the gray industrial carpeting.

<I'll demorph first,> Ax said. <In case there is need for defense.>

In a few minutes, we were in our normal forms. With our keen Andalite, hawk, and human senses.

It was then I wished I was still a roach. A roach would not have seen so clearly what I saw now.

In the corner of the room was a small, portable Yeerk pool. Like a stainless-steel Jacuzzi. The steel-bound briefcase I'd seen that morning was nearby.

On the lip of the portable Yeerk pool was a large clamp. A sort of collar.

My mother's neck was in that collar. It held her tight. It held her head sideways, so that one side of her face, one ear, was pressed into the water.

The rest of her body stood awkwardly, help-lessly, bent over.

<The Yeerk is feeding,> Ax said coldly.

A Yeerk must return to the Yeerk pool every three days to absorb Kandrona rays. Otherwise it starves.

The complex box was a portable Kandrona.

My mother was, for this time, for just these few moments, my mother. The Yeerk slug that was Visser One was out of her head, in the liquid, feeding.

Right now she was my mom.

Five steps and I would be beside her.

I moved.

CHAPTER 10

<Marco!> Tobias snapped.

A second step. A third!

<Ax!>

Suddenly there was an Andalite tail blade at my throat.

I stopped.

<No, Marco,> Ax said calmly. <Visser One will be back in your mother's head the second she senses any danger. And you could not open those locks with force. They are no doubt controlled by a brain-wave interface. So that the Yeerk can maintain control, even outside your mother's body.>

I grabbed his tail and tried to shove it away.

But an Andalite tail is nothing but one long, coiled muscle. It moved about three inches.

<Marco, stop it!> Tobias said. <Back off and think about it! Right now she's turned away, so she can't see you. You step into her line of sight, she'll *know*.>

I stopped trying to push Ax's tail away.

<We're here to investigate, Marco,> Tobias said gently. <Not the time, my friend. No matter how much you want it to be, this isn't the time.>

<What if you fail, Marco?> Ax asked. <If you reveal yourself but are unable to stop the Yeerk from reentering her. What then, Marco?>

My mother was locked into a vise, three feet away from me. Maybe Ax was wrong. Maybe I could release the clamp. Maybe . . .

I stepped back.

I felt like dirt. She was right there! Free, if only for a moment. I could tell her I was okay! I could tell her . . .

Nothing. I could tell her nothing. Ax was probably right. I would not have been able to free her. Visser One would reinfest. Security would be breached. Our secret revealed. And then?

And then we would have to destroy the inno-cent as well as the guilty.

It made sense. It was the cold, calculated, smart thing to do.

I wiped my hand over my face. It came away wet.

"What's that? In the corner," I whispered, distracting myself.

<Surveillance and communications equipment.>

It was a console about the size of an upright piano. On top sat a satellite dish, pointed toward the outside window. In the middle of the console was a large screen. And on that screen were images that seemed to have been shot from above.

Images that were disturbingly familiar. Images of free Hork-Bajir.

<Visser One knows about the Hork-Bajir colony,> Tobias said grimly. <That's what she's up to.>

<Handheld Dracon weapons over there, surveillance devices, a portable Yeerk pool,> Ax observed, looking around the room with his stalk eyes. <Everything the Visser needs for guerrilla action.>

<That briefcase, by the side of the Yeerk pool,> Tobias said. <Is that what she was carrying this morning, Marco?>

"Yeah. And there's another one on the desk by the window," I whispered.

<Emergency Kandrona Particle Generators,> Ax surmised. <One use each. It appears the Vis-

ser only has six days to finish whatever it is she's started.>

"Rot in hell!"

It was said softly, but ferociously. We froze.

My mother's voice! But who was she talking to? To us? Did she know we were there? Had she heard us?

No. No, of course: She was talking to the Yeerk. It must have begun to reinfest her.

BBWWBBWWBBWW!

The room started to tremble. I jumped, startled out of my trance.

<What?> Tobias demanded.

"Out of here!" I hissed.

We darted through a second door. Into a small, private bathroom.

BAM!

Even in the bathroom I felt the shock of the blow. Someone or something slamming the office door with the force of a battering ram.

BAM! BAM!

"The Yeerks," I said. "They're here to kill her!"

<Then they will be doing our job for us,> Ax answered coldly.

"Not while I stand around and watch," I said.

<The person in the next room is not your mother. It is Visser One. She will kill you the first chance she gets.>

I ignored him. Gorilla. It was my favorite power morph and I was ready to bust some heads. If I couldn't save my mother from her Yeerk, at least I could save her from whoever was trying to kill Visser One.

<You are being extremely foolish,> Ax said.

"Bull. You're letting your hatred of Yeerks get in the way. If Visser Three is trying to kill Visser One there may be an opening for us."

<An opportunity?> Tobias said thoughtfully.

<Maybe,> Ax allowed. <But Prince Jake said we were not to —>

"Blame me," I muttered.

<We will,> Tobias said with a laugh.

FWAM!

The outer door crashed in.

TSEEEW! TSEEEW!

The familiar sounds of Dracon beams firing!

I opened the bathroom door. In the office, total chaos.

The Visser had freed my mother's body from the pool and she was crouched behind the surveillance console. She was firing a Dracon beam.

A Hork-Bajir was staggering back, a burning hole in its chest. But more were pushing through the doorway.

<Party time,> I said, now fully gorilla.

I opened the bathroom door and barreled out.

Visser One shot a surprised glance at me. She hesitated. Should she shoot?

Two huge Hork-Bajir rushed her. She turned her attention back to them. Too late!

A bladed arm swung. It was meant to remove my mother's arm. It missed and knocked the weapon from her hand.

She was helpless. The Hork-Bajir leaned close.

WHUMPF!

My fist flattened the snout of the Hork-Bajir. He staggered back. Visser One dived for her Dracon beam. Ax leaped from the bathroom.

"Andalite!" one of the Hork-Bajir yelled in shock.

FWAPP!

Ax's tail blade did to the Hork-Bajir what he'd intended doing to my mom.

But the Hork-Bajir were still coming. There were four in the room. More outside.

"Tseeeeer!"

Tobias flapped, talons out. A flurry of russet feathers and the Hork-Bajir fell back, clutching his eyes.

We fought our way through the stunned aliens, smashing and slashing. And then, out of the corner of my eye, I saw Visser One level her Dracon beam. At *me*!

Too far away for me to reach her. <Ax!> I yelled.

FWAPP!

The bullwhip-fast tail slammed the portable Kandrona and knocked it into her head.

<Rather stupid, Visser, since we are attempting to save your life,> he said to her.

"I don't take help from Andalites!" she screamed in rage. But her weapon was out of reach. Hork-Bajir blocked any hope of retrieving it.

The Visser turned and ran into the bathroom.

I jumped to my feet, just in time, for an injured Hork-Bajir flailing blindly was about to cut a deep gash in my side. I grabbed it by one of its bladed arms and flung it into a wall. I sunk my fist into a second Hork-Bajir. And Tobias did his own damage. But it was Ax who was winning this fight. His tail was whipping left, right, too fast for the eye to follow.

The Hork-Bajir fell back before him. Fell back fighting at first, then in panic. They fought to get back out through the door.

I grabbed the splintered mess of door and shoved it back in place.

I gave Ax a look. <Dude. I think you really scared them.>

<We obviously took them by surprise,> he said modestly.

<I hear chopper blades,> Tobias said, hawk head cocked.

<Is it a getaway, or reinforcements?>

<Don't know. Marco. Open that window for me.>

I picked up a chair and threw it against the window. It shattered. <In high-rise office buildings the windows don't open,> I said.

Tobias flew out through shards of glittering glass. He reported immediately. <They're outta here!>

"Die, Andalite!"

The bathroom door flew open. An arm was raised. A frail-looking arm. With a not-at-all-frail-looking Dracon beam.

She'd stashed a weapon in the bathroom!

TSEEEW! TSEEEW!

The light beams were aimed dead-center at Ax. But Ax wasn't there by the time she'd pulled the trigger.

I dove for the floor and shot forward, sliding on spilt Hork-Bajir blood. The Visser was crouched behind the surveillance console again, hate in her eyes. In my massive fist I grabbed one of the Visser's enormous briefcases and blocked a shot aimed at my head.

With all the power of my gorilla muscles and all the rage of a kid bent on revenge, I leaped forward, tumbled over the surveillance console, and onto Visser One.

WHHUMMPPFFF.

Four hundred pounds of muscle and flesh crushing my mother's slim human body.

I stood up, yanked her to her feet, calmly disarmed her, and tossed the weapon aside. I put her in an armlock.

A gentle armlock.

<We save your regrettable life and you try to kill us,> Ax sneered. <You are a perfect representative of your species.>

"So why don't you kill me?" Visser One spat. "Arrogant Andalite filth! Why don't you kill me now?"

<As you wish,> Ax said, nodding to me. <For my part I say: Kill her.>

CHAPTER 11

<Kill her now,> Ax said in public thought-speak.

But in a private aside, heard only by me and Tobias, he added, <I am speaking only for dramatic effect, of course. But it would be good for the Yeerk to be frightened.>

I tightened my grip. Let her feel the irresistible power in my arms. I resisted the urge to cry, "I'm sorry, Mom!"

"Stop!" the Visser screamed. "Don't kill me!"

I relaxed my massive arms. My mother's human body slumped. I could hear her labored breathing. See her shoulder blades through the thin silk blouse she wore.

<Why shouldn't we kill you?> Ax taunted. <You Yeerks killed my brother, Elfangor.>

"Elfangor's brother! I might have known some branch of his squalid, cowardly family still lived! But it was Visser Three who ended Elfangor's evil life. He's the one you want. And so do I. I want him dead as much as you do. Not that I wouldn't have been proud to claim Elfangor as my own victim."

<I'm going to let her go,> I said. I couldn't hold her any longer. I was halfway between a loving hug and a furious strangle.

<She may still have concealed weapons,> Ax said privately.

<Hey, I am not frisking my own mother.>

<She's not carrying anything,> Tobias said. <I'd see it.>

I let her go. She straightened her blonde wig and took a few deep breaths.

I knocked the wig from her head with a sudden backhand. I don't know why.

The Visser . . . my mother . . . shot me a look of cold amusement. "Gentle Andalite warrior," she said mockingly.

<You're alive. So be quiet,> I snapped.

"I won't be alive for long," she said, suddenly weary. "Visser Three had accused me of treason. Now, once his Hork-Bajir report, he'll have the proof he can take to the Council of Thirteen.

They've issued a *gashad*. A warrant to kill me on sight."

Tobias flew over to the photographs we'd seen earlier. <What were you up to?>

She laughed. "And wouldn't you like to know its every detail."

<Yes, we would,> Ax said. <And you will tell us. Or you will die.>

"I'm already dead."

<Your plan must involve discrediting Visser Three,> Ax said. <We might help. If it were Visser Three with the *gashad* on his head, your own head would be more secure.>

Her dark eyes glittered. "You help me destroy Visser Three, then you destroy me. Is that the plan?"

<Yes,> I said bluntly.

She laughed derisively. "The truth. You do me the honor of not taking me for a fool."

<And if you get the chance you will destroy Visser Three, and then us,> I said.

She leaned close, bringing her face so close to mine. "Yes, I will."

<Now, Yeerk,> Ax said, <you will tell us your story. I would advise hurrying. Visser Three's forces will be back.>

I watched as my mother's body straightened. Her voice was calm, unemotional.

"I had returned to Earth to construct an underwater facility. It would produce a host body useful for the invasion of Leera. But, as you Andalites know, that facility was destroyed. I was disgraced. I was demoted to sub-Visser rank. But Visser Three set out to complete my destruction. He told anyone who would listen that I was a traitor. The Council of Thirteen believed him and issued the *gashad*. I have been in hiding ever since."

<Yet, here you are, on Earth. Seemingly alone,> Ax said. <No doubt there is a ship in orbit. And perhaps a Bug fighter hidden here on the planet. No doubt you have more of the emergency Kandrona generators on board.>

The Visser shook her head. "I'm not leading you to my ship, Andalite."

Before I knew what I was doing, before I had time to think, I snatched up the portable Kandrona and slammed it hard on the floor.

<Tell her "ticktock," Ax,> I said.

"A good tactical move," the Visser said. "Shorten my time. Make me desperate. But it won't work."

<We'll see,> I muttered.

<What is your plan, Yeerk?> Ax pressed. <What information do you have on Visser Three that could redeem you in the eyes of the Council of Thirteen?>

62

Visser One relaxed my mother's body against the shot-up surveillance console. For a moment she looked as innocent as a third-grade teacher about to tell a folksy story about the young Abe Lincoln.

"Free Hork-Bajir," she said simply. "Visser Three has allowed escaped Hork-Bajir to start a colony right under his nose."

<But the Yeerks have enslaved the entire Hork-Bajir population,> Ax replied. <There are no free Hork-Bajir left in the galaxy, much less here on Earth.>

"Don't play dumb with me," the Visser said. "It's the one thing we admire about you Andalites: your intelligence."

<Where did you get this theory of yours?> Ax demanded.

"That's my business." Visser One shrugged. "There are all sorts of ways to figure out what is going on underground if you have the mental acuity, which Visser Three most assuredly does not. Tell me Andalite," the Visser continued. "How did your brother, the mighty Elfangor, succumb to so flawed and incompetent a Yeerk as Visser Three?>

<I could ask you the same thing,> Ax replied, calmly.

"I know the importance of revenge to the

Andalite culture," Visser One said. "Visser Three killed your brother. You are honor-bound to kill him. I can make that happen."

<For a price,> Ax said.

"For a price," she agreed.

<What price?> I asked.

"The Hork-Bajir colony. Give me the free Hork-Bajir. I will give you Visser Three."

CHAPTER 12

A moment of silence.

<Tell her we agree,> I told Ax privately.

Tobias erupted. <Are you insane! There's no way we're giving up the Hork-Bajir!>

<No, we won't. But she doesn't know that. She thinks we're Andalites. You know the one word Yeerks always use in describing Andalites? Ruthless. That's what they think. She'll buy it.>

Ax said, <That is all you ask, Yeerk? The free Hork-Bajir?> He laughed. <I was concerned you might demand something of value.>

"We have a deal?"

Ax said, <Tobias?>

<You had so better know what you're doing, Marco my man,> Tobias said to me. <This is way beyond anything Jake and the others have approved. We're doing a deal with the enemy.>

<You want Visser Three?> I shot back. <She can give us Visser Three.>

<And then she replaces him,> Tobias said. <I know Ax's motive here: He has a personal score with Visser Three. The question is, do you have a personal problem here as well?>

<It's good strategy, Tobias. You know I'm good at that. You know I'm good at seeing the main chance.>

<Yeah. You are. But that's your mother.>

I couldn't argue with that. <Jake left it up to you, Tobias.>

Tobias laughed without any humor. <You'd better not be playing us, Marco. If it comes down to it, Visser One . . . no matter what host body . . . is meat. You know that, right? You're clear on that.>

<I'm clear,> I said.

<Okay, Ax-man,> Tobias said.

<We have a deal,> Ax said.

"Tell me where to find the free Hork-Bajir!"

<You will be given that information when the time comes,> Ax said. <Once Visser Three is exposed, I will kill him. That way, you will have not

committed treason by murdering a full Visser and I will have achieved my sworn revenge.>

"One more thing: You and the rest of your gang will be there. I will need you to help me eliminate the free Hork-Bajir. I am one person, all alone."

Ax started to answer. I stopped him.

<Agree, Ax.>

<What?> Tobias demanded.

<Alone my butt,> I said. <She has some kind of force. She's too calm. Too relaxed about Visser Three trying another attack here. She already has her forces nearby. Agree to what she asks.>

<A Hork-Bajir is a Hork-Bajir,> Ax said indifferently. <No more than animals to us.>

"Contact me when you are ready," she said.

<How?>

She smiled then. A smile that was my mother's smile. Again I felt the opposite urges: to cry and to destroy.

"I have E-mail." She laughed and told us the address.

Then she narrowed her eyes and looked at us, each, one after the other. "One of you does almost all the talking. Two of you stay in morph. Visser Three is a fool. He has overlooked something strange about your group of rebels. He has missed something."

67

She grinned a savage grin. "But don't worry. When I am returned to power I will figure it out. And then . . ." She made a gun hand, pointed it at my head, and said, "and then . . . TSEEEEW!"

CHAPTER 13

We left. We demorphed in the stairwell and climbed the stairs the hard way. As soon as we reached the roof Tobias took to the air to catch a look around.

<Four helicopters on the way,> he reported. <They'll be here in five minutes. Visser One will have a bunch of Visser Three's Hork-Bajir down on her before she knows it.>

"Let's get wings," I suggested to Ax.

Moments later we all three took to the air. It was hard flying. No updrafts, no thermals at night, just dead air you have to flap your way through like a bat.

We flew through the tall concrete and steel forest. Here and there a single light, or the lights of an entire floor burned. I saw cleaning people pushing wheeled trash cans and vacuums.

One light illuminated a room full of tired-looking men and women eating pizza and standing around some kind of chart.

It's strange, but flying near tall buildings always makes you feel like you're higher up. You notice the altitude, I guess, when you realize you're flying past the fortieth floor or whatever.

No one said anything till we were clear. The clatter of helicopters was loud behind us.

I was confident that Visser Three's troops would find an empty room.

<Well, Marco, you've just agreed to betray Jara Hamee, Toby, the entire Hork-Bajir colony. You'd better have a plan.>

<I do.>

<Gonna tell us about it?>

<We're going to take them both down. Vissers One and Three,> I said. <They want to kill each other, we'll help them.>

I could sense Tobias's hesitation. <You're setting up your mom?>

<No. I'm setting up Visser One.>

<Marco, she's —>

<Shut up, Tobias,> I snapped. <Okay? I know all about it. You guys don't think I'll do it? Well,

here's a news flash: I'll do it. Me. Not any of you. Me. My plan, okay?>

<You don't have to prove anything, dude,> Tobias said.

<It's not about proving anything. It's about winning this stupid war.>

<We must speak with Prince Jake, of course. Inform him of what we have learned. Obtain his approval of your plan.> Ax, of course.

<It's the middle of the night. We can't get to Jake right now. Not with Tom home. We'll talk to Jake tomorrow. Right now, we act.>

Tobias shifted his wings, moving slightly away. I swear, I've never met anyone who could express disapproval the way Tobias can.

But at that moment I didn't care what Tobias thought. Taking control, doing, would keep me from dwelling on it. From falling apart.

I knew Tobias and Ax were doubtful. I knew they didn't entirely trust me. They thought I was playing a double game. But they were wrong. I had seen the way to destroy both Vissers. I had seen it in all its perfection.

People don't understand the word *ruthless*. They think it means "mean." It's not about being mean. It's about seeing the bright, clear line that leads from A to B. The line that goes from motive to means. Beginning to end.

It's about seeing that bright, clear line and not caring about anything but the beautiful fact that you can see the solution. Not caring about anything else but the perfection of it.

That's what had happened. I saw the way to take both Vissers down. And that's all that mattered.

But I wasn't going to explain all that. Other people's pity just messes with the straight line. Other people's pity makes you think things you can't think about when you are seeing the line.

<Look, we're gonna need to acquire an animal native to mountaintops. But I'm not a zoologist, so we go see Cassie.>

<It's the middle of the night where Cassie lives, too,> Tobias said.

<Yeah, but she doesn't have a Controller in the house with her,> I said.

<We do not know that for certain,> Ax pointed out.

<If you guys want to bail, fine. I can do this alone.>

A bluff. I knew they'd hang with me. Tobias had no choice. He could either try and stop me forcefully, or go along.

<You're a jerk, Marco,> Tobias said.

<Yeah, I love you, too,> I said.

CHAPTER 14

The night was peaceful as we flew.

I knew in my heart that four chopper loads of Hork-Bajir had burst into an empty office and found no one. Knew it. I don't believe in destiny. But I felt destiny this time.

We would meet, Visser One and I. We would meet on a mountaintop. And I would end it all there.

Only a few stars shone high in the sky through the thinning clouds. We flew closer together than we ordinarily would during the day, when the sight of three birds of prey grouped together in the sky would attract unwanted attention. We flew from downtown to uptown, across the neighborhood where Jake and I and Rachel live, out past more suburbs, and into the almost country where Cassie's family has their home and the Wildlife Rehabilitation Center.

We landed in a large, leafy tree whose branches gently scraped Cassie's bedroom window. Tobias moved close, walking the comical sideways bird walk, like a parrot in its cage. He tapped on the window with his beak.

TAP. TAP. TAP.

<She's not moving,> he said.

<Is she in there?> I asked.

<No, it's after midnight, so naturally she's out in the yard playing Hacky Sack,> Tobias snipped.

He was ticked at having control taken from him.

<Hacky Sack?> I said.

<Hacky Sack?> Ax echoed.

<Everyone shut up!> Tobias said in exasperation.

<Tap louder.>

<Gee, do you think, Marco?>

TAP! TAP! TAP!

<Nothing. Must be dreaming about . . .>

TAP! TAP! TA-CSSSHHHH!

The glass shattered. It fell in a shower of glittering shards.

<Oops.>

"Jake?" Cassie bolted upright in bed.

<Awww, isn't that sweet?> I said, so Cassie

74

could hear. <Her first thought is "Jake." Makes you wonder just what kind of dreams she was having.>

<Cassie, it's us,> Tobias said. <Sorry about the glass.>

"I'm going to have to explain this you know," Cassie said, rubbing the sleep out of her eyes. Then, belatedly, she snatched modestly at the neck of her sleep shirt.

<Just say a bird hit the window,> Ax suggested. <You would not be lying.>

"That would be a change from routine," Cassie muttered. "What are you guys doing?"

<Checking out babes,> I suggested.

"Marco, what are you all doing here? What happened tonight? Is anyone hurt?"

<We are unhurt,> Ax said.

<We need a good morph for traveling in the mountains,> I said. <Something that can climb. Something with some size, if possible. Some ability to inflict punishment.>

"You better not have woken me up and broken my window to —"

<Kind of a ticktock situation, here —> I interrupted.

Cassie looked doubtfully at Tobias, then Ax.

<Marco has a plan,> Tobias said dryly.

"Jake?"

<Cassie, just help us, okay?> I said.

75

She sucked in a deep breath. "Okay. Mountain goat."

<Good! A goat from The Gardens' petting zoo. What could be easier to acquire?>

"Not that kind of goat, Marco." Cassie shook her head. "A mountain goat. Sharp horns. Amazing agility. A hind-leg kick that could send a person through a barn wall. Those guys can weigh almost three hundred pounds."

<Fine, fine,> I said. <Where do we get one?>

Cassie hesitated. "Is he okay?" she asked Tobias, referring to me.

<Seems to be.>

"Tobias, this is a stressful situation for Marco. Jake put you in charge. If Marco is —"

<Hey! Hey! Am I invisible? I'm here, okay?>

"Okay, then. I'll ask *you*. Are you okay, Marco? You seem kind of jazzed. Manic."

I said a harsh word. Then, <Everyone stop acting like I'm some kind of dimwit. I know what I'm doing. I don't need a bunch of psychoanalysis, here. This isn't *Oprah*!>

Cassie bit her lip thoughtfully. She got a distracted look in her eyes. I realized she was listening to Tobias or Ax or both communicating in private thought-speak. I don't know what they told her. But I saw that flicker of emotion in her eyes: pity.

"Well," she said at last, "The Gardens has a

newish mountainside habitat. It's open-air so you shouldn't have any trouble getting in after hours. Or getting near the goats."

I launched from the windowsill. Neither Ax nor Tobias spoke to me as we traveled. Maybe they were privately ripping me apart. I didn't care.

I saw the bright, clear line.

CHAPTER 15

The Gardens: Kick-butt amusement park meets zoo. Very expensive admission price. If you go in through the gate.

I spotted the darkened Ferris wheel ahead, and my favorite, the snaking, sloping roller coaster in the amusement park section of The Gardens. A moment later, flying over the zoo, I saw what had to be the mountainside habitat Cassie'd told us about.

A rolling, grassy plain. A stream meandering across the north end. And in the middle of the plain, an imposing, incredibly steep stone and concrete "mountain" full of shallow caves and terraces. The habitat itself was surrounded by a high mesh fence, on top of which we landed.

I could make out the dim, humped shapes of several goats just inside the largest of the shallow caves. They were sitting on the ground in a cluster. Several more goats stood motionless, staring back at the three large birds staring at them.

<Interesting,> Ax observed. <Bearded, white-coated creatures with hooves. And horns. Grazers. I would point out the similarities between the mountain goat and Andalites, except for my extremely disappointing experience with the cow.>

<I think mountain goats might be a bit more intelligent than cattle, Ax,> I said. <And a bit more aggressive. These guys look like they mean business.>

<Look at the shoulders on that one staring at me,> Tobias said nervously. <He's like a line-backer or something.>

<Yes, acquiring one might be quite a challenge,> Ax observed. <Perhaps we should choose one that is asleep.>

<Good idea.> I lifted off and flew to a ledge outside a small cave. Tobias and Ax followed. I'd seen one large shape inside. Yup. A big mountain goat, asleep. Male? I couldn't tell. All of the

goats had black horns and beards though I figured some had to be female.

Ax and I demorphed quietly a few feet away.
The fake mountain hadn't looked like all that
much when we were birds. As a human, though,
the ground looked a long way down.

I swayed and grabbed some rock.

Then I began to crawl over toward the massive, shaggy white beast.

"What if he wakes up?" I said.

<This is your little picnic, you tell me,> To-
bias sniped.

I sighed. "Tobias, look, get up off my back,
okay? I know you're thinking Jake will blame you
if this all goes bad. But we need to just get along,
here, okay?"

Tobias laughed. <Okay. I'm done pouting. Unless we end up getting kicked cross-country by
these big goats. Then I'll pout plenty.>

I stepped closer. Dumb to be scared of a goat.
All the animals I'd been near. All the animals I'd
been, and I was worried by a goat?

I placed my hand on its side. It looked at
me.

"Please don't shove your horns into my kidneys," I said pleasantly.

It stirred. I wanted to pull back. But that
would have been the wrong move.

My hand touched rough fur. I focused. I needed to begin acquiring this big boy right now.

The goat seemed about ready to spring up and butt me into the next dimension. But then it settled down as the acquiring trance took hold.

Ax clopped forward and when I withdrew my hand, he laid his own on the goat. Tobias was last.

<Come on, you guys,> he said when he'd hopped off the back of the sleeping goat. <Morph and let's get out of here before it wakes up.>

"Uh, don't look now but I think we have another problem."

On the ledge stood Mr. Mountain Goat's homeboys. And they didn't look happy to see us.

"Uh-oh," I said.

It took the goats approximately two seconds to cover about a hundred feet of ledges, boulders, gullies, and curves.

I turned.

I ran.

Tobias fluttered away to safety. Ax leaped nimbly away. Me? I got goat horn in the butt.

I flew.

"Aaahhhhh!"

Later, I read that male mountain goats enjoy

butting each other with their horns — in each other's butts.

And let me just say that unless you have been butted down a fifteen-foot-high cliff by a two-hundred-and-fifty-pound angry male mountain goat, you have not experienced true humiliation.

CHAPTER 16

I lay in my bed, in the dark. Every few minutes I'd check the glowing numbers of the clock. Three fifteen. Three forty-two. Four-oh-nine.

I wanted to sleep. Needed to sleep. Couldn't.

Ever have one of those nights? Where you're exhausted, where you'd pay anything just to fall asleep? But the wheels in your head just keep spinning and spinning and spinning?

Imagined conversations. Me talking, explaining, arguing. Changing the words around, repeating them, rehashing them. Around and around in circles.

Me talking to Jake, an imaginary Jake. Explaining, with perfect logic.

Me talking to my dad in some fictional future, some nonexistent world where things were different and I could at last tell all the secrets I'd guarded with my life.

Me talking to my mom. Raging. Explaining.

Me explaining to my mom, as my *mom*, as my *real mom*, why I had to do it.

Me explaining to my mom as *Visser One*. Laughing, chortling, savoring my victory over her.

This is how I defeated you! I crowed.

This is how I saved you! I explained.

No choice. No choice.

I had to do it, Dad, you understand, right? What else was I going to do? Too much on the line. I had responsibilities. You know how that is, right? And besides, she was already dead to you. You'd already grieved, remember? You spent years just sitting in your chair, staring blankly, your life falling apart . . .

See, Jake? Don't ever doubt me again. I did it, okay? I put the mission first. I saw the big picture. So just don't ever doubt me again, because I did what had to be done. . . .

Mom, what was I supposed to do? I saw all the plays. I saw all the pieces on the chessboard. There was no solution that freed you. There were only solutions that destroyed you. I had to. How else? How else to . . .

Die, you Yeerk piece of crap. Wither and die, and remember with your last, dying thought: It was for her. I killed you for her.

For Jake.

For my dad.

For . . .

Around and around, as the hours ticked away. As exhaustion sank deep into my bones.

Someday, if we won, if humanity survived, we'd be in the history books. Me and Jake and Rachel and Cassie and Tobias and Ax. They'd be household names, like generals from World War II or the Civil War. Patton and Eisenhower, Ulysses Grant and Robert E. Lee.

Kids would study us in school. Bored, probably.

And then the teacher would tell the story of Marco. I'd be a part of history. What I was about to do.

Some kid would laugh. Some kid would say, "Cold, man. That was really cold."

I had to do it, kid. It was a war. It's the whole point, you stupid, smug, smirking little jerk! Don't you get it?

It was the *whole point*. We hurt the innocent in order to stop the evil.

Innocent Hork-Bajir. Innocent Taxxons. Innocent human-Controllers.

How else to stop the Yeerks? How else to win?

No choice, you punk. We did what we had to do.

"Cold, man. The Marco dude? He was just cold."

CHAPTER 17

The next morning we all met at the barn. I was past tired. My butt was sore. My elbows were raw from skinning down the artificial cliff.

Tobias seemed tired, too. Too tired even to tease me about my encounter with the goat. Ax acted as though he'd spent the night snoozing like a baby.

I explained my plan to Jake and the others.

"We take out Visser One. We take out Visser Three. We leave the Yeerks believing they've erased the free Hork-Bajir colony. The free Hork-Bajir end up much safer; the Yeerks end up leaderless."

I avoided looking at Cassie. From Jake there

was just the briefest flicker of sadness. But Jake, too, is addicted to the bright, clear line.

Rachel kept her eyes down, focusing on the dirt-and-hay floor.

Rachel's not stupid. She knew anything she said would just make me mad. And I guess she, like all of them, was putting herself in my shoes. Wondering if she could do it.

"If it works, we have them both," I concluded. "But there's a lot to go wrong. A lot of unforeseen things that —"

Cassie put a hand on my arm. "Marco, you know we'll try to help your mother, in whatever way we can."

"She's only one person." I shrugged off her hand and stood up. "And we're supposed to be saving the world, right?"

It was one of the lines I'd practiced the night before. It sounded more bitter and less cool and calm and in control than I wanted.

"Okay," Jake said.

That was it. Just "okay." He didn't come out with any of the lines I'd put in his mouth in my imaginary conversations.

"So we do it?" I asked.

"Yeah. You call the plays, Marco."

I sucked in a shaky breath. "Okay. Okay. Okay, we want to push the timing. Don't give Visser One time to think about it. Keep her off balance. I know the place. I hiked near there once with my dad. I need someone to contact Erek."

Erek is one of a small group of Chee. They are androids. Pacifists by programming. But working to infiltrate the Yeerk ranks. Spies.

The Chee pass as human by the use of so-phisticated holographic projections. They live human lives. Many human lives. They've been on Earth since the time of the pyramids.

<I'm on it,> Tobias volunteered, flying down from his perch in the hayloft.

"Okay. We don't let her see us. We play the ar-rogant Andalites the whole way. Visser One can't —"

"She's your mother!" Cassie exploded. "She's not 'Visser One.' She's your mother! Is everyone just going to let this happen?"

Jake sent her a cold look. "This is not the time, Cassie."

"When is it going to be the time? When Marco's mind is screwed up forever by this? He's in denial. This is his mother, for God's sake."

Jake said nothing. No one said anything. Cassie's words just hung in the air.

"Go on, Marco," Jake said finally.

"We want her to focus on disliking Andalite arrogance," I said. "She hates Andalites. So, we want her to dwell on that. Maybe it will be enough to keep her from seeing the trap. As soon as we're ready, I'll E-mail her."

"Ax, do you think we can play the roles of arrogant Andalites?" Jake asked.

<It will certainly require good acting skills to imbue the fundamentally humble and dispassionate Andalite character with a taint of arrogance,> he said.

"Yeah. *Humble* is the very first word that comes to mind when I think 'Andalite,'" Rachel said with a drawl.

<I think I should do as much of it as possible,> Tobias suggested. <I spend the most time with Ax. I can do a pretty good "arrogant Andalite.">

<I am very close to taking offense,> Ax huffed.

"Okay, Tobias. But you have to allow time to get to the mountains."

<I'll have a tailwind. And I go "as the bird flies," not on winding mountain roads.>

I went to the computer Cassie and her dad use to keep medical records. "Ax? We need a secure screen name. Something not even the Yeerks could trace back here."

Ax worked at the computer for a few minutes, muttering about primitive human technology. Muttering in a dispassionately humble way, of course.

<You may compose your message.>

90

I typed. I hit "send." I didn't think about what I was setting in motion.

"Okay. Everyone understands what's what, right?" I asked.

"Yeah."

"Okay. I'm outta here."

I began to morph to osprey. Moments later, I was in the air. Relieved to be away from my friends.

Approximately fifteen minutes later, I landed in a leafy elm tree near the busy corner of Green and Spring Streets.

Tobias sat on a telephone pole across the street, preening his feathers.

<You get Erek?>

<Yeah. He's on it. Think she'll show? Your m —. I mean, Visser One?>

<Yeah. I think she'll show.>

Minutes later she drove up in a rented Audi. She slammed it into a parking space, bullying her way past a family in a Chrysler Town and Country.

She climbed out. The driver of the van yelled something at her. She gave him a look. He decided to drive off.

She wasn't in the disguise, anymore. She looked like my mom again. She was my mom.

The olive skin. The shampoo-commercial black hair. The dark eyes.

<Visser One,> I told myself.

She stood pretending to be fascinated by the wares displayed in the window of the Ace Hardware.

<You're on, Tobias,> I told him. <Remember: arrogant Andalite.>

<Visser One, you will follow my instructions literally and immediately,> Tobias said.

Her head jerked. She looked around. She eyed a blind woman's guide dog suspiciously.

<You will be crossing paths with a human-Controller named Chapman,> Tobias said.

"Chapman!" she mumbled. "One of Visser Three's incompetents. He would turn me in in a second if it meant his advancement through the ranks."

<Exactly the point, Yeerk. You want Visser Three. Surely you understood that we had to attract his attention. We are delivering him. Do not question me again.>

My osprey eyes could see her mouth form a string of foul words. Tobias ignored her.

<Chapman's afternoon run takes him past the human business called Dunkin' Donuts. It is one street to the east. Walk there now. Make sure he sees you. Do not attempt to escape,> Tobias said. <We will protect you, if necessary.>

Visser One was standing outside Dunkin' Donuts at 1:55 P.M.

At precisely 2:10 P.M., Chapman rounded the corner, dressed in a lime-green and yellow jogging outfit.

The Yeerk in my mother's head opened her hand. Her purse dropped. Chapman, always playing the role of pillar of the community, bent to pick it up for her. He straightened and held out the purse.

Visser One formed a smile. Then, the smile froze.

It was convincingly done.

Chapman said nothing. But I could see the blood draining out of his cheeks. He took a step back and then ran off double speed.

From my next perch, on the corrugated tin roof of Fred's Car Wash, I saw Chapman stop at a pay phone a block away and frantically punch the numbers.

Visser One stood fuming. She looked around again, trying to spot us. But there were pigeons and dogs and we could have been anywhere.

<Walk north one street,> Tobias said. <Embark on the large vehicle that stops at the next corner. Disembark at JCPenney.>

"It's called a 'bus,' you Andalite fool," she muttered in response. I happened to hear as she passed by below me.

Tobias's act was working.

<Good job, Tobias. You do a good Andalite. When the bus comes, you fly. I'll ride.>

<You're the boss,> Tobias said.

Two minutes later a bus pulled up against the painted yellow curb.

<Embark,> Tobias snapped.

<Embark?> I asked Tobias.

<I thought it sounded like something Ax would think was right.>

My mother got on the bus. I swooped down off the car wash and landed, scrabbling, on the hot metal roof of the bus. There was nothing to hold on to. But a couple of tiny rivets had popped out and I seized a precarious hold by prying my talon tips into the holes.

Not my favorite way to travel.

The bus rumbled back into traffic and began the five-minute ride to the mall. Fortunately it never got over ten or fifteen miles an hour. Ducking my head down and streamlining my body, I could resist the wind.

I could have kept pace from the air, which would have been a lot more comfortable.

Two blocks away from the stop in front of JCPenney, I lifted off. I flapped for altitude. An osprey near the ground sticks out.

I scanned the area for familiar faces. I spotted the hard stare of a peregrine falcon's eyes.

Jake was perched atop a bank out on the periphery of the mall parking lot.

<We're on schedule at this end,> I reported.

<You're sure Chapman saw her?>

<Oh, yeah, he saw her. He nearly wet himself.>

<Good. Were you followed?>

<We can only hope.>

<Any sign of her own forces?>

<We haven't exactly had time to watch everyone,> I said. <How about the others?>

<Rachel and Cassie are in place. Ax should be getting to the mountain soon. I think we can be confident that Erek will be there, on schedule.>

<Okay, Tobias?> I called.

<Yeah, I'm above you.>

<You can go, dude. We got it, here.>

<I've got it, here,> Jake corrected. <Don't forget, Marco. You stay quiet.>

<I know, I know,> I said, a little exasperated. <Don't let her hear my voice. Not even the one in my head.>

<That's right. The clothes are in that Dumpster.>

<You had to stash them in a Dumpster?>

<Hey, you wanted clothes, right?>

I flew to the Dumpster. It wasn't bad. I think

it was all boxes and stuff from the Gap and Old Navy. Much better than a restaurant Dumpster.

I demorphed in the Dumpster and pulled on the clothes Jake had stashed there.

Jake landed beside me.

<Fly, right?>

<That's the plan.>

Jake quickly demorphed, then morphed to fly. He buzzed his wings, took a few quick turns, then landed on my shoulder.

I climbed out and we hurried around to a side entrance of the JCPenney.

Visser One had walked from the bus stop through the door. She waited impatiently for instructions. She pretended to shop, tugging fitfully at some kids'-size Michael Jordan jerseys.

My size, maybe. Was she thinking about the son her host body had once had?

No, not likely. She was thinking about the fact that Controllers were everywhere. Thinking about the fact that by now Visser Three had a tail on her. Was watching her. Tightening his ring around her.

I lurked behind a tall potted plant. "Okay, directly ahead," I whispered to Jake. "There's a TV screen hanging down from above. Do you see it?"

Flies are very weak at seeing distances. It's why I had to be human. So I could act as an air traffic controller and direct Jake toward his target.

<I see bright, swirling lights, above and straight ahead.>

"That's the TV. Okay, she's in an almost straight line from here to the TV, just a shade to the right."

Jake took off. I lost sight of him immediately, of course. Hard to see a fly against the confused backdrop of visuals.

<I'm on her,> Jake announced a few moments later. <Beginning contact.>

Seconds later I heard Jake's thought-speak voice, sounding very different. And I saw my mother's head snap up.

<Go to the back of this establishment, Yeerk,> Jake instructed. <Purchase a neck protection garment. Also artificial skin designed for the protection of hands.>

Scarf and gloves. I almost laughed. It was classic Ax-ese.

Visser One must have said something harsh. The next thing I heard was Jake saying, <Do not be foolish, Yeerk. We are using this process to equip you as necessary. And to discover any pursuit. For your information we have spotted four human-Controllers who are already watching you.>

A lie, of course. But Visser One's head snapped around before she got control of herself.

<We are creating a trail, Yeerk,> Jake said with utter smugness. <And you are being watched, so do not attempt anything stupid. One wrong move and we'll kill you now and worry about Visser Three later.>

<Very nice,> I complimented Jake.

<Next stop, the camping store,> Jake said. <Let's see how well she holds up. She's volatile. She could go off.>

<No. She'll stick with the plan,> I said.

I understood Visser One. She saw the bright, clear line, too. Problem was, only one of us could be right.

CHAPTER 18

Rachel, her hair in two dorky braids and a goofy fisherman's cap low on her head, was staked out in Shoes and Handbags.

I was a few aisles over, in Hosiery. I looked slightly out of place. I could only hope that no one from school would spot me as I perused the racks of sheer-to-waist, sandal-foot taupe panty-hose.

That's the kind of thing that stays with you in school.

Visser One stormed into the Scarves, Gloves, and Hats department. She grabbed a gray wool scarf off a shelf, snatched a pair of woefully inadequate fancy leather gloves, and dutifully purchased them with a no-doubt-fake credit card.

Then she started to walk back toward the exit leading into the mall. All according to plan.

Then . . .

"Excuse me, ma'am? Could you follow me please?"

A security guard. Plainclothes. The kind of guy who always seems to end up following me through a store.

Rachel shot a glance at me. She raised a questioning eyebrow.

I moved closer, carefully, keeping out of Visser One's line of sight.

"Follow you?" my mother's voice snapped. "Why?"

"Just follow me, ma'am. I need to ask you some questions."

The Visser's hand drifted down toward her purse. The guard saw the movement, too.

"You are under arrest for stealing that scarf."

"I bought this scarf," the Visser said tightly. "I have the receipt."

The guard laughed nervously. He glanced around, like he was looking for help. But he sounded determined enough. "If you reach into your purse for the Dracon beam I'm sure you have, I will kill you right here and now, traitor."

Visser One's hand was in the purse.

The guard reached inside his coat.

100

We were about two seconds away from a shoot-out in a crowded store.

Suddenly Rachel was behind me. "Hide, you idiot. You're gaping like a tourist! I have this," Rachel whispered.

She was right. I was standing in the open, drawn toward her without realizing it. If my mother had turned . . .

I ducked behind a display of long velvet shawls.

Rachel moved fast. She locked her hand around Visser One's wrist. Then, in a loud, nasal whine, she said, "I saw you buy that scarf!"

The guard hesitated. Visser One stiffened. She stared closely at Rachel, but Rachel had turned away.

"This woman is being arrested, and she didn't do anything! Lady! Lady! You sold her that scarf, now she's being arrested! What kind of a store is this?"

One thing we couldn't do: leave any Controller behind who could recognize us and wonder. Rachel was avoiding eye contact, hiding beneath her hat and bad hair. Hiding behind a false voice.

I hoped it was enough.

"It's ridiculous! This woman is being arrested and she paid for it! She paid too much, if you ask me, for that fabric. It's not cashmere, after all!"

I smothered a grin.

It was working. A crowd was gathering. The saleswoman was in it now, agreeing that Visser One had paid for the scarf.

<What is going on?> Jake wondered, confused.

It's hard to follow conversations when you're a fly. But of course we couldn't answer him.

Rachel moved out of the crowd and grabbed my arm.

"Let's get out of here."

"No one is watching —"

"Security cameras," she hissed. She nodded toward the ceiling. I saw the dark glass blister that hid a camera.

"Oh."

I followed Rachel toward a dressing room.

My first and probably last visit to a women's dressing room.

Rachel led me out a back door. Into a maintenance walkway, all cinder block and steel doors.

We reached the camping store before Visser One and Jake did. Cassie was waiting there.

She ran interference as Visser One was put through her paces buying climbing rope and pitons.

Rachel and I drifted around, pretending to shop. We were watching the others in the store. Watching those who were watching Visser One.

Jake had bluffed earlier, claiming that we'd spotted four human-Controllers on Visser One's tail.

That was no longer a lie. Within minutes we were confident that the true number was not four, but five.

"You wanted to make sure she was followed, Marco. She's being followed. And now we are setting up one heck of a shoot-out at the OK Corral," Rachel whispered. "You'd sure better know what you're doing."

"Yeah. I'd better."

CHAPTER 19

She had ropes and pitons, gloves and boots.

She had a tail of human-Controllers behind her as she drove the rented Audi from the mall out of town, toward the distant mountains.

The OK Corral.

All of us were in the car with the exception of Tobias and Ax.

We were in roach morph, crawling beneath the driver's seat.

Fuzzy black carpet was like tall grass beneath my six legs. A long-forgotten, open roll of peppermint Lifesavers was a huge log, its diameter far longer than we were tall.

Way, way overhead, as high as clouds, was the steel tube and coiled spring underside of the seat. Too far away to see more than huge, indistinct shadows were gigantic feet and ankles pressing on high-rise pedals.

She knew we were with her. She didn't know where we were, but she knew we were watching her.

"Why don't we merely take a helicopter to this Hork-Bajir colony?" she asked.

<You assume the colony is located somewhere high up?> Cassie took over the job of communication. We needed to put Visser One off her guard. Needed her to begin to see us as allies. Cassie was the one for that job.

"Obviously," Visser One snapped. "Am I a fool? Ropes? Pitons?"

<You would not find it from the air. It is in a narrow, hidden valley high in the mountains. Trees would block a simple human helicopter.> She paused. <Your troops, when they arrive, will need to cut their way in.>

"My troops?"

<We are not fools, either,> Cassie said. <You do not intend to merely arrest or discredit Visser Three. You intend to kill him. We both know that with his morphing ability he is far more powerful than you, with your unstable human host body.>

"I can deal with Visser Three."

<Can you? We have tried many times. And yet, he still lives.>

105

"Humility? From an Andalite?"

<Realism from an Andalite,> Cassie said.

Visser One barked out a laugh. "You're afraid of him."

<Tell her, "yes,"> I said privately to Cassie. <Tell her he's killed a lot of us.>

<Yes. We were far more numerous, once. Many of us have died fighting Visser Three.>

A lie, of course. But it sounded real enough. Visser One would latch on to the information. She would think we were fools for revealing it.

We wanted her to think us fools.

"Do you imagine I will be more gentle when I am in power, again?"

I started to tell Cassie what to say. But she was already there, ahead of me.

<No. We simply think you will be weaker,> Cassie said. <The disruption of command will work to our benefit. And in direct battle you will be easier to kill than Visser Three. Humans, Controllers or not, die easily.>

Again, it had the feel of honesty. The insult would make it seem honest.

And it had the added benefit of focusing my mother . . . Visser One . . . on the danger of Visser Three. We were reminding her just how deadly Visser Three could be.

"And yet . . ." Visser One mused. "And yet, the

casualty reports from Earth are always weighted heavily toward Hork-Bajir and Taxxons. In fact . . . I am trying to recall when I have ever seen a report listing a human-Controller casualty."

My guts were ice.

We had made a mistake. We had made a terrible mistake.

<What do I say?> Cassie demanded.

<I . . . I . . .> My brain wouldn't work. The thoughts wouldn't form into any sort of order.

Visser One had just put her finger on our greatest secret.

<Say *something*!> Rachel yelled.

<No, too late,> Jake interrupted. <Too late. Let it go. No choice.>

"Well, well, well," Visser One said.

She knew.

There was only one reason why a group of Andalite guerrilla fighters would inflict more casualties on Hork-Bajir than on humans: The Andalite guerillas weren't Andalites.

A human would spare a human life.

<She knows,> Jake said. <Or at least suspects.>

<Yeah.>

<Marco . . .>

<Nothing changes,> I said harshly. <She was going down before. She's still going down.>

Not true. Before it had all been abstract. It had all been about the solution, the line from A to B.

Now it was about survival. No one could know the truth about us. It would bring our annihilation.

No one could know what we were, and live.

CHAPTER 20

Visser One drove like a madwoman. The Audi tore around hairpin mountain curves at speeds that would have been high on a freeway.

The roll of peppermint Lifesavers had become a menace. With every wild turn or braking it rolled suddenly, a redwood log coming downhill at us.

<Has your mother always driven like this?> Rachel asked.

<My mother is not driving,> I said coldly. But she was. My mom *had* always been a wild driver. It used to make my dad crazy. This was the Yeerk tapping into the human host's brain.

<Maybe so,> I amended. No need to start a

109

fight with Rachel. <Maybe that *is* the way she used to drive.>

<Yeah? Now I know where you get your driving skills.>

Rachel, being nice. I laughed to myself. When Rachel started being nice it meant things were really bad.

Visser One took a hard right and the ride turned bumpy.

An understatement.

The carpet jumped beneath us. We used our roach legs as shock absorbers, but there was a lot of shock to absorb. Wild vibrations that translated to the roach mind as danger.

Suddenly, mercifully, the car stopped.

"I have followed your directions. Andalites," she said.

The final word was said with a half laugh.

<We must be at the Visitors' Center,> I said.

<Good,> Rachel said. <I'm carsick.>

<Unpack the items you purchased. Begin to walk along the main trail.>

"Visser Three's forces will be all over me in seconds!" she protested.

<No. They'll track you,> Jake said. <They won't move till he himself is here.>

"Tell that to the fool back at the mall!"

<He acted out of panic. He wasn't expecting you.>

Visser One got out of the car and slammed the door. We waited until enough time had passed for the Visser to grab her gear from the trunk, change into the hiking boots, scarf, and gloves and start up the trail.

<Let's go,> Jake said. <Rachel? You're first. Keep low.>

Rachel motored out from under the seat onto the back floor mat. She began demorphing immediately, growing, sliding, shifting to keep her mutating limbs from being caught in the tight space back there.

Mostly I saw her feet. They filled my vision. Bare, of course. We'd never learned to morph shoes.

Her head eventually rose above the seat back. "Okay," she said. "We're clear. For now."

<Okay. Morph and go.>

Rachel tried to roll down the window. But of course it was power, and Visser One had taken the keys. She cracked the door on the passenger side. She morphed to bald eagle and took off, racing to her appointed position.

If Tobias had not made it, Rachel would. If both made it, so much the better.

Cassie, Jake, and I spread out throughout the car and began to demorph. If we'd all stayed in one place and demorphed we'd have ended up as sardines.

I demorphed on the passenger side. My head rose from the gruesome mass of bug exoskeleton. I could see through the windshield. Really see. Like a human.

She'd chosen a parking space distant from the few other parked cars. Good and bad for us. No one would spot us on the way to their own car. But we'd have a long, open walk to the trailhead.

I looked around. Rachel was just clearing the nearest trees.

I spotted Visser One moving speedily toward the trail. She'd always kept in good shape, my mom. Although sailing had been her thing, not hiking.

Jake was in the driver's seat. "Okay. We go straight to bird morphs. The bad guys won't be far behind us."

"Or far ahead, either," I said, nodding toward the dwindling figure of Visser One.

"One at a time or we'll look like a bird-of-prey convention," Cassie said.

I began to morph to osprey. I was closest to the open door. A few minutes later I was all feathers and talons. I fluttered out through the door, landed on the gravel, and flapped into the air.

I wasn't ten feet up before I saw it: a long, black limousine. It was entering the parking lot.

No one goes camping or hiking in a limo.

<Visser Three!> I said. <Heads down. He's here!>

I continued flapping, flapping, fighting dead air, feeling conspicuous.

Not that there weren't birds of prey in the forest. But Visser Three knew by now to look out for hawks and eagles.

The limo skidded to a stop, spraying gravel. Behind it, three big SUV's.

The limo window rolled down. I was maybe thirty feet up, forty feet downwind from the Audi.

A hand thrust out of the limo window. Osprey eyes saw it clearly. Saw what it was holding.

<Jake! Cassie!> I yelled.

TSEEEEEW!

The Dracon beam fired. The front of the Audi sizzled, fried, and disintegrated.

<NOOOO!> I cried.

TSEEEEEW!

Ka-BOOOM!

A fireball exploded from the Audi's gas tank. The entire car, what was left of it, erupted upward, spun halfway on its axis, and landed on the gravel.

It was a charred shell before it hit the ground.

CHAPTER 21

<Jake! Cassie!>

No answer. Nothing. Silence. Silence but for the crackling of the fire.

<Rachel!> I yelled. <Jake and Cassie are . . . I think . . .>

But Rachel was already out of thought-speak range.

Slam! Slam! Slam!

Doors opened and closed and the human-Controllers piled out of the SUV's. Boots hit gravel.

Chapman climbed out of the limo and joined the guys coming from the SUV's.

And then, last, came a human who was no human.

Visser Three in human morph.

He looked around, barely sparing a glance at the burning wreck of a car. A park ranger was running from the Visitors' Center.

The Visser jerked his head.

TSEEEEW!

The ranger sizzled and disappeared.

Then, I felt those cold eyes on me. At this distance his voice was faint. If I'd been human I'd never have heard my death sentence.

"The bird," he said. "Kill the bird."

TSEEEEW! TSEEEEW!

To my left! To my right!

The Dracon beams scorched the air on either side of me.

Two seconds for them to aim again. One, one thousand . . . Two, one thousand . . .

I jerked left.

TSEEEEEW! TSEEEEEW!

Misses, far to one side. And now I was farther away. The nearest tree was only fifteen feet away.

TSEEEEEW! TSEEEEEW!

Just in front of my face branches burst into flame.

I flared, lost speed, and dropped. I used the momentum of my fall to whip hard around the tree trunk and zoom wildly, inches off the pine needles.

The Yeerks wouldn't get another shot at me. Not now.

Oh, God. Jake! Cassie!

The burning car was burning right inside my brain. The aluminum skin had been evaporated, leaving nothing but the bones of the car. Bare aluminum posts and fire.

And, though I had not seen them except in my imagination, the singed, heat-cracked bones of my friends.

What now? I asked myself. What now?

The plan. Was there still a plan?

I tried to think. But I could no longer see the bright, clear line. All I could see was flame.

Visser Three. I'd been so busy worrying about Visser One I had forgotten that he was our main enemy. I'd intended to harass and trick and distract Visser One into carelessness. But I had tricked myself.

Visser Three was going to win. He was going to kill my mother. And he would not die. He would kill her, and he would not die. I would have set up my own mother for murder by my own worst enemy.

No. No. That couldn't be. I had to think. Had to think.

Tobias, maybe. Rachel, maybe. They were the next step.

Ax. Where was Ax? Clearing the place of campers? Scouting the location?

Where? What were they doing? How . . .

Show me the line, I begged. Show me the A to B.

My friends. My mother . . .

All my fault. And now I was lost. Nothing to do but stand and watch the horrible drama play out.

No. No, the awful voice in my head said. The line was still bright and clear. The plan still worked. If Ax and Erek had done their jobs the plan could still work.

Only one thing needed to be changed: I would have to play the part of Jake.

CHAPTER 22

I flew ahead to the appointed rendezvous. I passed over Visser One on the way. She was still moving quickly up the hill. Had she heard the explosion? Did she feel the fear eating at her, the fear that death was coming up behind her?

Or was she filled with anticipation? Was she giddy and energized with the thought of killing her foe, of annihilating the free Hork-Bajir, of living to dance on Visser Three's grave?

I pulled far ahead. I headed for the clearing halfway up the mountain. There was a cluster of lean-tos for campers on the edge of the clearing. Ax, using his morphing ability, should already have frightened them from the area.

We didn't want innocents caught in the cross

fire. We didn't want bystanders hurt. That was our plan.

<Tell that to that ranger back there, Marco,> I said to myself. <Tell it to his family. No innocent bystanders in our little war. No place for them, is there? No time to think about the damage you do with our bright, clear line.>

A campfire smoldered below. In one of the shelters two sleeping bags were spread over bunk beds. Two backpacks sat propped against the wall. These nature lovers had left in a hurry.

Ax at work. Maybe. Or maybe Visser Three's forces had come in from this direction as well. More innocents. Dead, or merely terrified?

We'd chosen Wildwood Trail specifically because it wasn't popular. It wasn't very scenic. It wouldn't be wall-to-wall crunchies working out their Timberlands.

And because, a mile or so up, we could cut away from the trail and go cross-country through terrain that would thin out the pursuit.

I spotted Visser One laboring up the slope, fighting the gravity I could easily defy. Her pretty face was dripping sweat. Her lungs gasped.

That was the plan, too. Too rushed, too scared, too tired to think. And yet, she already knew too much. She'd figured out what Visser Three had not.

It was weird, perverse, maybe. But I was

proud of her. As if it had been my mother, and not the Yeerk in her head, who had penetrated our deepest secret.

I caught an updraft and soared high into the air. Up into the clean, clear air.

I wanted to keep flying. Just catch a breeze and sail away and leave it all behind. But how could I? How could I, with the possibility of Jake and Cassie being dead?

<No, no, Marco,> I sneered. <Far better that they should die to bring about more death. Yes, that would give their lives meaning.>

I rose high and searched the trail ahead. But not even osprey eyes could penetrate the dense foliage. I did not spot Ax or Tobias or Rachel.

Below, far back down at the trailhead, Visser Three was still in his human morph. He was moving swiftly up the trail. A dozen armed men before him, a dozen more behind him.

But one man was out in front, all alone, moving very fast. He wore a camouflage jacket and blue jeans. A camouflage stocking cap was pulled down, hiding most of his red hair.

The way he was moving he was either an athlete or a very experienced woodsman. He left the trail and went cross-country.

Either going ahead to take a shot at Visser One. Or going ahead to spy out what was happening.

I'd have to watch Red-hair. He made me nervous.

I knew that what I saw was not even the thin edge of Visser Three's true forces. I knew that the sky above me was dotted with shielded Bug fighters. And maybe the Blade ship as well. Not to mention any of Visser One's loyal troops.

The killing had only taken a ·rest break. It would start again once Visser Three was sure of Visser One's goal. Once all her forces were in the open and committed. Once he was sure of victory.

I circled back to the campsite. Visser One had been instructed to wait there. I floated down, skimmed in, hidden from the Visser's sight. I landed in the middle branches of a tall pine.

Only then did I see the goblin form of a Hork-Bajir, standing perfectly still. So still it could have been a statue.

<Rachel? Tobias?> I called.

<Rachel,> she answered. <Haven't seen Tobias, yet.>

<I'm here,> a thought-speak voice answered. <Right above you, Marco.>

I jerked my head upward. The seven-foot-tall, bladed form rested comfortably another twenty feet up the trunk.

<You guys forget: Hork-Bajir are arboreal. Why be on the ground when you can have some altitude?>

<Where are Jake and Cassie?> Rachel asked.

I didn't answer. I couldn't.

<Marco?> Rachel pressed.

I couldn't. Couldn't say it.

<Marco!>

<Visser Three. He got them.>

<What?> Tobias cried. <Captured?>

<No. No. I don't think so.>

CHAPTER 23

We waited. Silent. Dangerous.

I know Rachel. I know she wanted action, not playacting. I knew she would explode at the smallest provocation.

I know Tobias. I knew that in the face of so much sadness he would retreat from his human side. I knew that he was more hawk now than ever, despite his Hork-Bajir morph.

And what could I say to them? What could I say to lead them? Or control them?

Nothing. Because I know myself, too. I knew that I was scared and desperate and that my insides were being eaten away. I knew that I was focusing all my mind, all my thoughts on the plan, the plan, the plan, shutting out all other thoughts.

I had nothing to say to Rachel or Tobias. They would do, or not do, whatever they chose.

Visser One wandered warily through the abandoned campsite. I saw her as Rachel saw her: the enemy. One of the Yeerk invaders who had cost her the life of her cousin and her best friend.

She was a dozen feet away, two long strides away, from Rachel's Hork-Bajir blades.

Rachel stepped into the open.

Tobias dropped easily from the tree, landing on T-rex feet.

My mother . . . Visser One . . . swung her backpack forward and reached inside. The Dracon weapon was in her hand in a flash.

I breathed.

Rachel was letting her live. For now. Fast as Visser One had been, she'd never have reached her weapon had Rachel not wanted her to.

"You . . ." Rachel said, stepping forward and speaking in the Hork-Bajir voice. "Where are Andalite friends?"

"Your friends are fine, Maska Fettan," the Visser responded.

"My name. You know my name," Rachel said, sounding relieved. Then, a slow Hork-Bajir scowl. "Andalite friends say password. All must speak password."

I spotted a movement so slight only a hawk would have seen it. Red-hair. Only the red hair was hidden now by the camouflage ski mask he'd pulled down over his face.

He was in a stand of bushes. Close enough to see. Not to hear. He had a Dracon beam in his hand. But the way he held it was for self-defense, not attack.

"Freedom now, freedom forever," Visser One recited with an amused sneer.

"Yes." Rachel smiled, if you can call what Hork-Bajir do when they're happy smiling. "You are friend."

"Yes. I am a friend to all free Hork-Bajir." The Visser could hardly resist masking my mother's face with a grin of glee. "How is the free colony faring, Maska Fettan?"

"Good, good! All free now. All happy. Much bark to eat," Rachel said.

"That's good. Love to hear that the bark is tasty," Visser One said, dripping contempt. "Now, conduct me to the colony, as you were in-structed to do."

"You change to bird. Fly. Human slow walker."

"Sadly, I am ill," Visser One said. She made a little cough. "I am unable to morph at the mo-ment. I will have to travel as a human."

"Human slow," Tobias interjected with true Hork-Bajir dimness.

"Yes, yes, it's all a mess," Visser One agreed testily. "I wish I could morph to bird and fly, but since that is not possible, perhaps you two geniuses could follow the orders you were given."

"Andalite friend says, 'Take her to colony,'" Tobias said.

"Yes," Rachel agreed.

"Up there." Tobias pointed off the trail. He pointed up toward a high, naked rock summit. "Up there is place. Up there Andalite friends hide colony."

A naked rock peak. The perfect place to stage a battle that would involve forces on the ground and in the air. The perfect place for an Animorph.

"Up there?" Visser One said slowly. Her eyes narrowed. "Holograms. Cloaking shields? Yes, of course. Few human interlopers, and camouflage and a force field would stop them. It would work. A small, deep valley most likely. Invisible from the ground because of the altitude. Easily concealed from the air or space by Andalite countermeasures. The energy drain would be immense, but not unmanageable. . . ."

I would have smiled. Yes, Visser One, just what I hoped you'd think.

Welcome to the OK Corral, Visser One.

CHAPTER 24

I'd seen enough. Visser One had fallen for it. So far.

Rachel and Tobias would handle the rest of the climb. It was unlikely the Visser would try to harm the two Hork-Bajir before she had been shown the way to the colony. Unlikely, but not impossible. She was armed. And I knew what Visser One was. Ruthless. Cruel. That she wore the face of my mother — the woman who had taught me about laughter — was a grotesque irony.

<See, *that's* ironic, Alanis,> I muttered to no one.

The ascent would take hours. Tobias and Rachel would have to slip away whenever possible to demorph and remorph. If Ax was nearby, on-station, it would work. He would substitute. One Hork-Bajir looked much like the next, but this substitution would be even more perfect than that. Some weeks ago, on a friendly visit with the free Hork-Bajir, Ax had acquired the same Hork-Bajir DNA Rachel was using. Not even a Hork-Bajir would notice any difference.

I drifted back down the hill. Back down toward Visser Three and his Controllers.

His force was growing. I don't know how they'd gotten there, but a force of Hork-Bajir was moving up the hill from the right flank, swinging through trees and marching along the ground. I counted thirty before I gave up.

This would complicate things. I'd hoped to isolate the two Vissers. Visser One, prepared as we had prepared her with ropes and pitons, would be able to climb. So would Visser Three who would simply morph something capable.

The jagged, naked rocks would delay the human-Controllers. But Hork-Bajir were strong. And, according to the Hork-Bajir we knew, they came from a planet where life existed entirely within impossibly steep canyons.

The Hork-Bajir-Controllers would be able to keep pace with Rachel and Tobias. Only a limited number of Bug fighters could be brought to bear within the limited space, so the balance of power on the ground was important.

Too much on Visser Three's side of the equation and he'd win without suffering much himself. And now, the wild card, we Animorphs, were reduced. Thirty Hork-Bajir-Controllers and a dozen human-Controllers, plus Visser Three. It was more than we could handle.

Far back down the trail, Red-hair rejoined Visser Three. So now Visser Three knew that Visser One had linked up with two Hork-Bajir.

Would he put it all together? Would Visser Three realize that these were free Hork-Bajir? That Visser One was on her way to the free colony?

It was getting to be time for me to change morphs. The air was thin, the updrafts nonexistent at this altitude. Flying was a chore. And soon I would stand out all too obviously.

<Where is Ax?> I wondered. <Rachel? Tobias? Have you seen Ax?>

<No,> Rachel said.

<He was supposed to do his best to clear the area then rejoin us,> I said in frustration.

<Plan not working out so well, General?>

<Just get Visser One up that mountain.>

<Face it, Marco, it's a fiasco. It's a total fiasco! We're dragging this woman up the moun-

tain for what? It'd be so easy to just give her a shove off the trail.>

<Shut up, Rachel!> I yelled. <Just shut up!>

<Oh yeah, you're calm and in control,> Rachel taunted. <Jake's gone. Cassie's gone. And the person running this mission is working on setting up his own *mother*? This is a waste of time. Marco, just fly off somewhere. Just get out of range so you don't have to see what I'm —>

<Rachel, that's enough,> Tobias said quietly.

I couldn't believe what I was "hearing." Tobias never messes with Rachel. I think Rachel was shocked, too.

<Marco has enough load on his shoulders,> Tobias said. <I trust him.>

<You trust him? You trust *him*?!>

<You just want Visser One?> Tobias said. <Or do you want them both? We need this woman alive as bait.>

All the while I could see Visser One scrambling over rocks, climbing, hauling herself up by roots and low branches. And Tobias and Rachel were with her, one ahead, one behind.

<Yeah, his plan's worked out so well so far,> Rachel said. But she fell silent after that.

I put her out of my mind. Besides, she was right. The plan was falling apart. I needed reinforcements.

Where was Ax? Where was the Andalite?

CHAPTER 25

I'd been a long time in morph. A quick check on Visser Three, and I would abandon the osprey.

Visser Three himself was still with his group of human-Controllers. They were slowing down, worn out by sliding in their street shoes.

But the Visser was no longer concerned with shoes. He had reverted to his Andalite host body. He was a nimble, dangerous deer.

No one was sweating more than Chapman. I almost felt sorry for him. But not too sorry. If all went well, my school would be needing a new assistant principal next week.

I circled behind them, staying out of sight as well as I could. I drifted close enough to hear scattered bits of conversation.

Some of it was very interesting.

"Let's kill her now," Chapman urged, gasping like a fish out of water. "Before they get away."

<Why, because you are weak and tired? No,> Visser Three said. <She is heading for the Hork-Bajir fugitives. I know it! Either to unite with them, or to prove their existence to the Council of Thirteen and discredit me. I will have her *and* the Hork-Bajir fugitives!>

"But, Visser, in these human host bodies, lacking equipment, we may be unable to keep up with you," Chapman said very respectfully.

<Am I blind? Am I a fool? Two columns of Hork-Bajir and Taxxons are even now converging. If you fall by the wayside, so be it. I will not be denied my victory!>

Evidently encouraged by Visser Three's seemingly tolerant mood, another human-Controller made the mistake of offering an opinion.

"It's hard to believe that these Hork-Bajir hosts could form a colony right under our noses. How did we —"

The Andalite tail blade whipped and stopped, quivering, pressed against the man's right leg.

"No, I —" the man cried. "I meant no criticism! No!"

"Visser, we need every man who can fire a weapon," Chapman intervened.

<Yes, you are right, Chapman,> Visser Three said. <It would be foolish to cut off his leg. How would he walk without a leg?>

The man almost had time to breathe a sigh of relief. Then Visser Three whipped his tail again. The man's left arm fell to the ground.

<You all will only hinder my progress,> Visser Three spat. <I will proceed alone from here. The Hork-Bajir and Taxxons will join us soon. And the fleet stands ready. Catch up when your frail bodies allow. I have a morph that will do very nicely for this challenge.>

With his entourage watching, Visser Three began to morph.

Squeeeeesh!

His Andalite head flattened to the shape of a B-movie flying saucer. His main eyes closed and sealed. His stalk eyes remained but thickened. The eyeballs bulged and reddened.

Multijointed legs sprouted from his sides. One, two, three — six, total, replacing his quick-disappearing Andalite legs and hooves.

His blue-and-tan Andalite fur seemed to be absorbed into him, as though it had been sucked in.

What remained was a translucent skin or shell of no particular color.

The legs lengthened, becoming spindly, almost like a spider's. The two front legs ended in claws. The back four legs ended in sharp, barbed spikes.

And then, before my startled gaze, the shell began to change. From a translucence that revealed vague, distorted blue, red, and orange shadows of his internal organs, it became green and brown.

It became the precise green of the trees overhead. The exact brown of the trail.

<A chameleon!> I whispered.

The Visser's bizarre, spindly land crab was nearly invisible, even to my eyes. The colors and patterns of its shell shifted as rapidly as it walked.

Okay, Marco, you knew he'd morph something dangerous. That still fits the plan.

Of course, I hadn't known he'd be nearly invisible.

CHAPTER 26

I landed and demorphed well off the trail.

Strange to be here, so high up. It was quiet. A few birds sang. The breeze rustled the sparse tall grass. The trees sighed.

"All I need is a picnic," I said, wanting to hear the sound of my own voice. "Some chips. A ham sandwich."

Jake and Cassie, burned in Visser One's SUV. Ax missing.

My mother . . .

I could run away. Leave town. Never come back. I had the powers. I could get by. I could go to Hollywood. Or France. Somewhere.

French Marco. I liked it. Were the Yeerks in

France? I didn't care. I wouldn't pay any attention to them.

"Oh, God," I moaned. I put my face in my hands.

<Marco! You are very badly located!>

My head snapped up. I looked around, confused, till I saw the northern harrier floating on the slight breeze.

"Ax?" I said, not that he could hear me.

<Marco, a column of Hork-Bajir and Taxxons is coming up the opposite side of this ridge. In approximately two of your minutes they will be able to see you.>

"They're not *my* minutes, you alien nitwit, they're everyone's minutes!"

But I was busy morphing. Not to osprey again. Wings were of diminishing usefulness now. But I still needed to be able to stay out in front of humans, Hork-Bajir, and whatever strange thing Visser Three had become.

Time for the goat.

Ax had floated lower. He kept to the air, but he could hear me now.

<I discern that the arrival of these additional forces so early in the plan may have created an imbalance that will affect our plans in a negative way,> Ax said.

"Gee, do you think?!" I yelled.

<We need reinforcements.>

136

"You know some private army you can call, 'cause if you do, now would be the time!" I yelled.

It was sarcastic. I didn't expect him to take me seriously. But before I could object, Ax had caught the breeze and was heading downhill, letting gravity give him speed.

"What the . . . What are you doing?" I screamed.

Insane! I'd found Ax and lost him within a minute!

"Okay, okay, get a grip," I told myself shakily. "Get a grip. Okay. Figure it out. Back to Rachel and Tobias and Visser One. The only thing to do. Morph. Come on, Marco, focus!"

I focused on the memory of the big mountain goat, asleep in its safe little zoo habitat.

Stupid, but I was ticked at that goat.

Morphing is never logical, never neat and clean and orderly. The changes don't necessarily start at the head and move on to the toes, though they can. And this time, they did.

Sprooot!

Two sharp, daggerlike black horns sprouted from the top of my head.

I felt an itchiness on my face. I raised my hand and felt a long, rather soft white beard beneath my chin.

The five toes on each of my feet melded together to form two big padded toes, toes that could spread to help the mountain goat keep its balance on snowy, rocky slopes.

White fur began to grow up my legs, which were becoming the stocky, sturdy back legs of the goat. Over the soft, fluffy fur grew coarser hair, protection against wind and rain.

Suddenly, I tipped forward. I fell on my hands, now also split hooves with rough pads underneath.

Screeeesh!

My small human shoulders heaved upward into the powerful, shaggy shoulders of the almost three-hundred-pound male mountain goat.

I felt the mountain goat's mind merge within my own. But I wasn't interested in fighting it. The goat wanted to climb, and so did I.

I bounded off across the sparse, rocky soil. Up, up, straight up.

The power in my legs was incredible! I wasn't climbing against the pull of gravity. Gravity was irrelevant! It didn't exist!

Up through the trees. Leaping easily, playfully over boulders that would have taken a human five minutes to clamber cautiously over.

My legs were pile drivers. I was on pogo sticks, just bouncing, bounding, springing, practically flying.

I spotted and smelled the Hork-Bajir as they

crested the ridge, but who cared? They'd never get me. This mountain was mine. These rocks belonged to me!

Up and up, pulling effortlessly away from the Hork-Bajir, I drew level with Visser One and my two friends. They had deployed ropes and pitons now. Visser One was being pushed and hauled like a sack of potatoes.

They climbed the easier path. I took a much harder way. A way with no trail, with scrappy miniature trees blocking my way, with no visible footholds, with tumbling gravel and crumbling rocks.

I went the way that no human climber, no expert rock climber armed with every piece of equipment could have climbed in under half a day.

It was an escalator to me.

My eyes spotted every minuscule crevice. My hooves caught every crack. I hauled three hundred pounds of goat up a sheer wall so easily that I might have been Tinkerbell floating upward on magic dust.

I passed Visser One.

Rachel spotted me.

<Marco?>

<Who else?>

<Yeah. Good luck, okay?>

<No problem-o, Xena,> I said.

CHAPTER 27

I waited atop the mountain, alone. King of the world.

From the peak, the back side of the mountain extended almost flat toward the west. All I saw was a long slope that extended perhaps a quarter of a mile before seeming to be broken by the spine of a ridge.

We had come up the east face. A nearly sheer drop. The southeast and northeast were no better — sheer cliffs.

A fatal fall in three directions.

A fatal fall for a human. Or human-Controller.

Nothing that looked remotely like a hidden valley. Nothing that looked remotely like a secret Hork-Bajir colony.

But then, that was to be expected.

My mother's face appeared very suddenly above the rocks to the east. She was being pushed up from beneath. She clambered up, clearly exhausted.

For a while she just lay flat on her back, gasping and coughing. Rachel and Tobias rose up behind her.

Then she rolled over and with sheer willpower made her body stand.

Once again I felt that strange pride. Even with Rachel and Tobias to help, it was an amazing accomplishment climbing this peak.

A fitting end. The last exertion, the last effort.

So easy for me now. I could throw my three hundred pounds forward, lower my head, slam into her, send her flying, arms windmilling helplessly as she fell and fell and fell . . .

The Visser would die.

His helpless host, my mother, as well.

"Andalite?" she panted.

<Of course,> I said. Be so careful, Marco, I warned myself. This was to be Jake's role. He was to talk to her. She can't know who you are.

But what did it matter now? It was over. It would end here.

It would matter because knowing at last that we had tricked her, she might call my name. She might say "Marco."

"Marco! Don't let them kill me, Marco!"

I shuddered.

I was lost. Her life would end here. So would mine, I now knew. How could I live? How could I live, knowing?

"Well, Andalite or human, or whatever you are behind that morph, you'd better know one thing: My loyal forces fill the sky! Betray me and you'll be blasted apart!"

<We have a deal,> I said blandly. <Visser Three will soon join us. He will be alone, or nearly alone.>

"The Hork-Bajir colony. I don't see any colony!"

<Erek,> I said privately, <I hope you're here, dude.> Then, in open thought-speak, <Not to get all *Prince of Egypt* on you, but . . . Behold!>

The ground of the western slope shimmered. Then it disappeared. Visser One actually jumped back. The valley appeared just before her feet.

"Hork-Bajir home," Rachel said, still playing her part.

Below us, beneath impossibly steep cliff walls, a lush valley teemed with free Hork-Bajir.

I watched the sick, eager smile spread across my mother's beautiful face as Visser One peered into the valley below.

Several young Hork-Bajir swung through the trees, playing a game of tag. Adult Hork-Bajir

142

stripped bark from the trunks of the tall pines. I counted at least forty or fifty Hork-Bajir going about their daily routine.

<Okay, we fulfilled our end of the bargain,> I muttered. <Now it's up to Visser Three.>

She smiled, right at me. "I know you. I know you, don't I?"

<I am an Andalite warrior. That's all you need to know.>

"No. Andalites don't make jokes. Let alone human popular culture references. No, you're a human. And . . ." She searched her memory, rolling her eyes up. "Someone I knew, once. Long ago, maybe. But someone I knew."

CHAPTER 28

I froze. Stiff. Still.

I wanted her to say my name.

I'd given myself away. Deliberately. I wanted her to say my name. I wanted her to call out to me, to say, "Marco, I love you, I miss you, I'm still your —"

Oh, God, I had messed up. The plan, I'd ruined it, just to hear her say my name. I'd been fooling myself. I couldn't do it.

<It's okay, Marco,> a gentle voice said. But not my mom. Rachel. <It's okay, man. It's okay.>

Then, everything happened at once.

Above the lip of the mountaintop he rose, grotesque, half sky-blue, half the color of bare rock.

Visser Three climbed up.

<Well, well, well,> he said. <What's this? Visser One perched on the edge of a free Hork-Bajir colony? Chatting amiably with two free Hork-Bajir and, unless I miss my guess, an Andalite?>

She spun to face him. No fear. "It's over, you incompetent fraud! My loyal ships are above us."

<So are mine,> Visser Three hissed. <And they will blow your ships from the sky!>

"So typical of you. You think only of brute violence. Fool. My ships are making a sensor record. They have recorded this valley, this colony of free Hork-Bajir! What do you think the Council of Thirteen will say when they see it?"

Visser Three showed no emotion. Most likely he couldn't.

Visser One reached into her backpack. Out came not a weapon but what looked a bit like a cell phone.

"This is Visser One," she said. "Attack!"

<Yes, by all means, attack me,> Visser Three said with a laugh. <My ships, too, are making a sensor record. A record of the traitor, the former Visser One firing on loyal Yeerks!>

Suddenly, the sky overhead seemed to part, like a cloth being torn at the seam, and there appeared a ship like none I had ever seen.

Huge! Larger than Visser Three's Blade ship.

It had eight pods arranged around a central, cylindrical core. Four massive engines bunched at the rear, blazing blue fire.

<A Nova-class Empire ship?> Visser Three gasped.

Just then, streaking out of the west, came a stream of smaller ships, Visser Three's Bug fighters. Visser One whirled to watch them, a swarm moving quickly across the back of the mountain range. Among them, a giant battle-ax: the Blade ship of Visser Three.

The squadrons flew low over the colony.

"Visser Three!" my mother yelled. "You are under arrest for criminal incompetence!"

<Traitor!> Visser Three roared.

He lunged, front claws snapping.

Visser One drew a Dracon beam.

Visser Three's Bug fighters sped toward Visser One's descending armada. The battle erupted. The sky was ripped by massive Dracon cannon firing, as Bug fighters and the Blade ship circled around Visser One's Empire ship.

Visser One fired.

Visser Three sliced.

<Aaaarrgghh!>

A sizzling hole appeared in Visser Three's color-shifting shell.

My mother screamed. She staggered and fell. Her clothes were stained red.

<NOOOO!> I cried. I leaped. Leaped at Visser Three, head down, horns ready.

<Marco! Stop!> Rachel cried. <It's the plan! It has to happen! It has to happen! She has to —>

<NOOOOOO!> I slammed into the chameleon morph. It jerked back. Visser Three staggered. Three legs crumpled.

Visser One fired.

The shot missed Visser Three. It hit me.

Searing pain. There was a neat semicircle of flesh gone from my haunch. I staggered, blinded and disoriented by the pain.

"Destroy the colony! The colony!" my mother screamed into her communicator. "Don't fire on Visser Three's ships! The colony! Kill them all! Kill them all!"

<Pathetic attempt. You can't hope to conceal your treason,> Visser Three said.

TSEEEEEEW! TSEEEEEEW!

Dracon cannon were firing from the sky above. The Empire ship was blasting the ground. Firing at what they thought was a colony of free Hork-Bajir.

A hologram.

Erek the Chee had created the illusion. And now, as the Yeerks fired, he created the illusion of Hork-Bajir burning, falling, dying.

But the laws of physics could not be denied.

The massive Dracon energies were not descending deep into a valley. They were hitting the mountain peak, only a hundred feet from us.

CRRRRRRR-ACK!

The ground shuddered.

And suddenly, the ground was falling away. A crack in the very rock itself.

A huge fissure opened up.

I staggered to my feet, crippled by the pain of my wound.

The fissure had separated us. Visser Three, and now an army of rushing, eager Hork-Bajir-Controllers on one side. Rachel and Tobias trapped there with them.

I was on the other side of the fissure. So was Visser One. My mother. We were alone.

She stood with her back to the cliff, raging.

"Too late, Visser Three! Too late to stop me!" Then, calling into her communicator, "Detach a fighter to get me off this rock!"

Rachel and Tobias were back against their own dead drop. Hork-Bajir hemmed them in, attacking relentlessly.

In seconds, it would be over.

All over. My plan. Done. Failed. Rachel and Tobias would die. Visser Three would live. And Visser One?

Out of the corner of my eye I saw a Bug fighter roaring out of the sky, rocketing down toward us.

I turned to face her. Visser One. The leader of the initial invasion of Earth.

She stared at me. She moved to aim the weapon at me.

I lowered my head and felt the power in my legs.

It would be a hundred-foot drop.

<I love you,> I whispered. And then, I lunged.

"The boy!" she whispered, amazed. "It's the boy!"

CHAPTER 29

I lunged.

The Dracon beam moved. Her finger tightened.

Too slow. She was too slow. I would hit her a split second before she could fire. I would hit her with all the power I possessed and she would fly backward into emptiness and —

RRRRROOOOOAAAARRR!

A flash of orange and black. It appeared over the lip of the cliff.

So fast!

The tiger hit me. Claws retracted, it hit me in my side and knocked me off my feet.

Spinning, I saw the Dracon weapon aimed right at me, following me, ready to fire.

And then, from the sky a bird dropped, wings folded back, talons out. It slashed at Visser One's face.

"Aaaarrggh!" she cried.

She clutched at bloody tracks on her cheeks. She staggered back.

<Mom!> I cried.

For a horrible long moment she teetered on the edge, fighting gravity. I leaped up, racing to grab her, pull her back, somehow, save her.

But the tiger wrapped a massive arm around me and held me down.

She fell. Disappeared from sight.

<No! No! No!> I cried.

<Hang on, Marco,> Jake said. <Hang on, man. Hang on, man.>

He held me that way, pinned down. The strength of his tiger morph made my own strength insignificant.

<Hang on, Marco. Hang on, man.>

Dimly, as though I was watching it on an out-of-focus TV, I was aware that battle raged on the opposite peak.

I knew that more Hork-Bajir had joined the battle. I knew that an Andalite was leading them. That they were pushing back the tide of the Visser's troops.

The free Hork-Bajir. Ax had brought them from the real colony, miles away.

In the sky a battle raged between the Empire ship and the Blade ship with its fighters. Not my problem anymore.

Nothing was my problem. All I had to do was listen to the voice in my head saying, <Hold on, Marco. Hold on, man. Hold on.>

CHAPTER 3O

I stayed in bed for most of the next week. Sick. At least that's what I told my dad.

I lay there staring at soap operas and Jerry Springer and old movies.

I didn't know how I'd gotten down off that mountain or made it home. I was gone during all that. Gone to a place in my head.

Jake came and saw me. He told me how Cassie had seen Visser Three's limo pulling in. They'd realized they were trapped. They'd gone at emergency speed back to roach morphs.

They figured nothing was going to kill a roach.

Cassie had been all the way into morph before Visser Three fried the car. Jake had only been halfway morphed. He'd been hurt, burned, unconscious.

Cassie had stayed to care for him, bringing him back to consciousness at the last minute. Just in time to demorph.

Jake had been seconds away from a lifetime trapped as something half roach, half human.

I listened to what he had to say. Listened to how Visser Three had escaped. How the free Hork-Bajir had lost five of their people in the battle.

I didn't care.

He went away and I flipped the channels with my remote control.

Two more days passed and Rachel came to see me. She sat in my chair and put her feet up on my desk.

"There's no body," she announced.

"What?" I asked distractedly. I flipped through a dozen more channels.

"Visser One. Your mother. I searched. In eagle morph. There's no body."

I felt my insides tighten.

"The Yeerks cleaned up their mess. Destroyed the evidence."

She shook her head. "No. The Yeerks Draconed the corpses. There are burn marks all over that hill. But nothing down where your mother fell."

The scene flashed back, another channel on the TV: the "my mother falling to her death" show. I saw her fall, slow-motion.

I saw the Bug fighter roaring past.

Could it have reached her?

No. Impossible.

"Nice try, Rachel," I said.

She shrugged. "I'm telling you what I saw. I wouldn't lie."

"Sure you would," I said. "Pity. Charity. Make Marco feel better."

"No. Because it won't make you feel better. It wouldn't be pity or charity. I wouldn't be doing you a favor. You've cried and yelled and hated yourself. It's bad, but if she's dead at least it would be over. If she's alive . . ."

I didn't say anything. She sighed and got up to leave. She touched the doorknob and I said, "Rachel? I was going to do it. Then I wasn't. I was trying to kill her. And save her. What do you do?"

"Do?"

"What do you do when you have to make a decision, and each choice is horrible? What would you do, Rachel? If it was your mom or dad or sisters. What would you do, Xena?"

"Me?" She sighed. "I guess I'd hope that someone would come along and take that decision away from me."

"Like Jake did to me."

"Yeah."

"What if she isn't dead? What if she really did survive? Oh, God, what if there's a next time?"

Rachel came back and sat beside me on the bed. She didn't hug me. Rachel's not a hugger. But she sat there with me.

"One battle at a time, Marco. One battle at a time."

Not much of an answer. But the only answer I had.

"Try the movie channel," Rachel said.

I aimed the remote control.

I came around the corner after school and saw a taxi parked out in front of my house.

My mother shot across the porch, suitcase banging against her knees, and hurried down the sidewalk to the cab.

What the . . . ?

My mom didn't take cabs. Nobody around here did.

Everybody had cars.

"Mom!" I yelled, jogging over. "What happened?"

Because something had definitely happened.

I mean, I've seen my mom sniffle at Save the Children infomercials and Hallmark cards, but I can't remember the last time I ever saw her really cry.

But she was crying now.

Something must have happened to Tom.

Or to my dad.

My knees went weak and wobbly.

Funny, how even when your whole life has shifted into a daily *Twilight Zone* episode, there are still some things that can make you panic.

"I left you a note on the fridge, Jake," she said, hefting her suitcase into the trunk and slamming it shut. "My flight leaves in an hour and the traffic —"

"Mom, *what happened*?" I blurted.

My voice was high and shrill, not exactly the voice of a fearless leader, as Marco would have pointed out, had he been there.

"Oh." She blinked away fresh tears. "Grandpa G died. His housekeeper Mrs. Molloy found him this morning. I'm meeting your grandparents and we're driving out to Grandpa G's cabin to make the funeral arrangements."

"Grandpa G's dead?" I echoed, trying to wade through the emotions whirling around in my head.

Grandpa G. Not Tom. Not my father.

"Yes. His poor heart just gave out," she said.

"You're going to the cabin?" I said. "What about us?"

"You'll be coming out as soon as your father clears his work schedule," she said, touching my shoulder, forcing a brief smile, and sliding into the back seat. "He'll tell you about it. Everything will be fine. Make sure your suit is clean. I'll call when I get to Grandma's. I gotta go, honey."

She slammed the door and waved.

I watched as the cab disappeared around the corner.

Now what?

I headed into the house. Checked the scrawled note stuck under an apple magnet on the fridge.

Yeah. Grandpa G was dead.

According to Mrs. Molloy, who'd talked to the doctor, his heart had stopped while he was putting jelly on a slice of toast. He'd never even gotten a chance to eat it.

I shivered.

I'd cared about Grandpa G and now he was gone, and my family was smaller.

I didn't like that.

The kitchen door burst open. Tom stormed into the room.

"And I'm telling you, Dad, I can't go!" he snapped, tossing his books onto the table and scowling at me. "What're you looking at?"

"You're home early," I said, surprised.

My father plodded in, weary, harassed, and closed the door behind him.

"So are you," I said, glancing from him to Tom. "Did Mom tell you guys about Grandpa G?"

"Yes," my father said. "I was hoping to get here in time to take her to the airport but the traffic was terrible. I saw Tom walking home and picked him up."

"Did you know we're supposed to go out to the cabin?" Tom demanded, glaring at me like it was somehow my fault.

"Uh, yeah," I said cautiously, trying to figure out what his problem was. "So?"

"So, Tom's already informed me that he doesn't want to leave his friends to attend his great-grandfather's funeral," my father said, looking at Tom, not me. "However, he doesn't have a choice. We're going. All of us."

"When?" I said, feeling like I was missing something important. It was there but I just couldn't grab it.

"We're driving up Saturday morning," my father said.

"Dad, I can't," Tom insisted. "The Sharing's expecting me to help out this weekend. I gave them my word!"

"Well, you'll just have to explain that something more important came up," my father said. "I thought The Sharing was about promoting family values, right? Well, we're going to pay our respects to Grandpa G as a family."

"Dad, you don't understand!" Tom argued desperately.

Why was Tom so dead set against going out to the lake?

Okay, so it was boring. Grandpa G's cabin was the only house on the lake. His closest neighbor had been Mrs. Molloy and she lived seven miles away, halfway to town.

The only other house around was an old, abandoned hunting lodge across the lake.

No cable. No Taco Bell. No streetlights or crowds.

No movies. No malls . . .

No Sharing. No Yeerks . . .

"Uh, Dad?" I said. "How long are we staying?"

"It depends on the funeral. I'll write notes so you'll be excused from school through Tuesday of next week —"

"What?" Tom's eyes bulged in shock. "Tuesday? Dad, no way! Four days? I can't stay away for four days!"

"You can and you will," my father said, losing patience. "We're going as a family and that's final."

Tom's throat worked. His hands clenched into fists.

And for one, brief second I had the crazy thought that he was going to attack my father.

And oh man, even though I couldn't morph in front of them, I could feel the surge of adrenaline that came right before a fight.

Three, maybe four days. The maximum time a Yeerk can last without a trip to a Yeerk pool is three days. Four days without Kandrona rays and the Yeerk in Tom's head would starve.

Starve, Yeerk. Starve.

"It won't be that bad, Tom," I heard myself pipe up. "The lake's nice, remember?"

It broke the stalemate.

Tom looked at me. "You're an idiot, you know that?"

He was playing his role as condescending big brother. I was playing my role, too.

Starve, Yeerk. Die in agony, die screaming, Yeerk.

"Shut up," I said. "I'm not the one who's being a big baby about leaving."

I said it to annoy him and to bring us back to the rhythm we knew, the kind of normal sniping I could handle.

Because the hatred in Tom's eyes when he'd looked at my father had scared me.

And the hatred that had flared up in me, the hatred of the Yeerk, the sick thrill of anticipating its pain, had scared me, too.

"That's because you have no life," Tom sneered.

"Oh right, and you do?" I shot back.

"More than you'll ever know," he said darkly, distracted now.

"Enough," my father said. "I'm going to change. When I get back we'll order pizza. How does that sound?"

"I'm not hungry," Tom muttered, staring at the floor.

I wasn't either but my father was looking at me expectantly, so I said, "Pizza, I'm there."

My father nodded, satisfied, and left.

I gave my brother a look of sympathy, making peace. "Maybe you can get out of it, someway."

I had to fight to keep the sneer off my face. *Or maybe, Yeerk, your cover is falling apart, maybe you'll have to choose between keeping Tom and keeping your filthy life.*

"Shut up," Tom said absentmindedly. The Yeerk had no use for me, no interest in me. I was dismissed. Irrelevant.

I turned and blasted out into the backyard, my mind already buzzing with the possibilities.

Tom's Yeerk was trapped. Under pressure. Squeezed. It wasn't ready for this turn of events. Didn't know how to play it out. Didn't know what to do.

An opportunity? Maybe. Yeah, maybe.

Die, Yeerk.

CAN JAKE WIN THIS FAMILY FEUD?

ANIMORPHS®

K. A. Applegate

Jake's brother Tom has convinced their father to attend a meeting of The Sharing. It seems as if Tom is going to force their father into involuntary Yeerk infestation.

The Animorphs don't know when or where the meeting is going to be held. And for the first time, Jake's quick-thinking mind freezes up. Jake is sure of one thing — he needs to save his father. But how can he do this without exposing himself and the other Animorphs?

ANIMORPHS #31: THE CONSPIRACY

K.A. Applegate

IN BOOKSTORES JUNE 1999!

Watch Animorphs on Television!

‹Know the Secret›

ANIMORPHS®

K. A. Applegate

❏ BBP0-590-62977-8	#1:	The Invasion	❏ BBP0-590-76255-9	#22:	The Solution
❏ BBP0-590-62978-6	#2:	The Visitor	❏ BBP0-590-76256-7	#23:	The Pretender
❏ BBP0-590-62979-4	#3:	The Encounter	❏ BBP0-590-76257-5	#24:	The Suspicion
❏ BBP0-590-62980-8	#4:	The Message	❏ BBP0-590-76258-3	#25:	The Extreme
❏ BBP0-590-62981-6	#5:	The Predator	❏ BBP0-590-76259-1	#26:	The Attack
❏ BBP0-590-62982-4	#6:	The Capture	❏ BBP0-590-76260-5	#27:	The Exposed
❏ BBP0-590-99726-2	#7:	The Stranger	❏ BBP0-590-76261-3	#28:	The Experiment
❏ BBP0-590-99728-9	#8:	The Alien	❏ BBP0-590-76262-1	#29:	The Sickness
❏ BBP0-590-99729-7	#9:	The Secret	❏ BBP0-590-76263-X	#30:	The Reunion
❏ BBP0-590-99730-0	#10:	The Android			

$4.99 each!

❏ BBP0-590-99732-7	#11:	The Forgotten
❏ BBP0-590-99734-3	#12:	The Reaction
❏ BBP0-590-49418-X	#13:	The Change
❏ BBP0-590-49423-6	#14:	The Unknown
❏ BBP0-590-49424-4	#15:	The Escape
❏ BBP0-590-49430-9	#16:	The Warning
❏ BBP0-590-49436-8	#17:	The Underground
❏ BBP0-590-49441-4	#18:	The Decision
❏ BBP0-590-49451-1	#19:	The Departure
❏ BBP0-590-49637-9	#20:	The Discovery
❏ BBP0-590-76254-0	#21:	The Threat

❏ BBP0-590-21304-0   ‹Megamorphs #1›:
The Andalite's Gift

❏ BBP0-590-95615-9   ‹Megamorphs #2›:
In the Time of Dinosaurs

Also available:

❏ BBP0-590-03639-4	‹Megamorphs #3›: Elfangor's Secret	$5.99
❏ BBP0-590-10971-5	The Andalite Chronicles	$5.99
❏ BBP0-439-04291-7	The Hork-Bajir Chronicles (Hardcover Edition)	$12.95

Available wherever you buy books, or use this order form.

Scholastic Inc., P.O. Box 7502, Jefferson City, MO 65102

Please send me the books I have checked above. I am enclosing $_____ (please add $2.00 to cover shipping and handling). Send check or money order–no cash or C.O.D.s please.

Name_____Birthdate_____

Address_____

City_____State/Zip_____

Please allow four to six weeks for delivery. Offer good in U.S.A. only. Sorry, mail orders are not available to residents of Canada. Prices subject to change.   ANI1298

http://www.scholastic.com/animorphs

Soccer Game Wednesday.
Math Test Friday.
Trip to the Yeerk Pool Saturday.
ANIMORPHS®
Life can be hectic.
Now you can get organized.
Animorphs® Student Planner 1999-2000
$9.95
Coming this June to bookstores everywhere.
WARNING: Don't let it fall into the wrong hands.
Animorphs is a registered trademark of Scholastic Inc. Copyright © 1998 by K.A. Applegate. All rights reserved. Printed in the U.S.A.
ANIP119

There's a place that shouldn't exist,
but does...

by K.A. Applegate

A new series from
the author of Animorphs.

Coming in June.